Dad

Mum

Luc

m

Lucy

Will

Dad

Mum

Luc

m

Lucy

Will

The Quigleys
in a Spin

Also available by Simon Mason:

The Quigleys
The Quigleys at Large
The Quigleys Not for Sale

The Quigleys
in a Spin

Simon Mason

Illustrated by Helen Stephens

David Fickling Books

OXFORD · NEW YORK

A DAVID FICKLING BOOK

Published by David Fickling Books
an imprint of Random House Children's Books
a division of Random House, Inc.
New York

Originally published in Great Britain by David Fickling Books, an imprint of Random House
Children's Books, in 2005.

DAVID FICKLING BOOKS and colophon are trademarks of David Fickling.

www.randomhouse.com/kids

Educators and librarians, for a variety of teaching tools, visit us at www.randomhouse.com/teachers

Library of Congress Cataloging-in-Publication Data
Mason, Simon
The Quigleys in a spin / Simon Mason; illustrated by Helen Stephens. — 1st American ed.
p. cm.
SUMMARY: The further adventures and misadventures of the four members of the Quigley family—
Mum, Dad, Lucy, and Will.
ISBN: 0-385-75098-6 (trade) — ISBN: 0-385-75099-4 (lib. bdg.)
ISBN-13: 978-0-385-75098-1 (trade) — ISBN-13: 978-0-385-75099-8 (lib. bdg.)
[1. Family life—England—Fiction. 2. Humorous stories. 3. England—Fiction.]
I. Stephens, Helen, ill. II. Title.
PZ7.M4232Qvm 2006
[Fic]—dc22
2005018482

Printed in the United States of America

10 9 8 7 6 5 4 3 2 1

First Edition

To Gwilym and Eleri

Contents

Dad's Big Toe

Dad's Big Toe

Dad was a hard worker. He had a little office upstairs, and he worked there all day and sometimes all evening. At night he was usually tired.

One night, Lucy and Will sat in their bedroom, watching Dad being tired as he searched for a story to read.

'You're all full of yawns,' Lucy said to him.

'The funny thing about yawns,' Will said thoughtfully, 'is they're not like sneezes.' He began to explain the difference between a yawn and a sneeze, but it was hard to hear him because he was lying squished face-down on the floor with his feet up on Lucy's bed and his head under the bedside table. Will liked to invent new positions.

'Will!' Dad said. 'What are you doing?'

'Relaxing.'

'Relax on your own bed,' Lucy said.

'I can't get my feet on the top bunk from here,' Will said, spitting out carpet fur. They began to bicker.

'No bickering,' Dad said. 'I'm too tired.'

'We're not asking *you* to bicker,' Will said. 'Lucy and I can manage on our own.'

'I mean I'm too tired to deal with you bickering,' Dad said, but he couldn't make himself sound cross because at that moment he began to yawn. In fact it was such a long, stretchy, blind sort of yawn that when it was over and he could see again, Will had finished bickering with Lucy and had gone downstairs to bicker with Mum instead, and the bedroom was quiet.

'Are you going to read to me now?' Lucy asked. 'Can you read if you're full of yawns?'

Dad sat on the bed, yawning. 'I'll try,' he said.

Five minutes later, as he was saying, 'For the first time in his life he was face to face with a silk-monkey,' he fell asleep. He didn't say he was going to fall asleep, he just did. He slid slowly sideways along the wall and sprawled on Lucy's bed with his eyes closed and his chin on his chest.

Lucy crawled out from under her duvet to have a closer look. 'Dad, you've fallen asleep,' she whispered.

Dad didn't disagree. Lucy watched him for a while. His face was slack and he was breathing through his nose in deep, whispery breaths. She put her finger out to feel the breaths, and they were warm and damp. She grinned to herself. Then she put her finger behind his right ear, and tickled him. A puzzled, frowny look went across his face, but he didn't wake up. Lucy grinned again. She tickled him behind his other ear, and in his sleep he smacked his lips together as if he were tasting something odd, and Lucy had to put her hand over her mouth to stop herself laughing. Then she sat back and looked at him a bit longer while she decided what to do next.

What would it be like, she wondered, if she tried to take his shoes off without waking him up? She thought it would be hard.

But it turned out to be easy.

Then she wondered if she could take off his socks without waking him up, and she did that too.

His bare feet dangled over the edge of the bed, and she sat looking at them, and grinning. His toes looked like small hairy animals dozing in a row. One wriggled in its sleep. Naturally Lucy thought about tickling them, but then she had a better idea. A much better idea. She got up and went to the drawer where she kept her precious things, and searched through it until she found what she wanted, and went back and sat cross-legged next to Dad's feet and got to work.

At first she found it difficult, and she made a few mistakes. It was hard to keep her hands steady all the time. But in ten minutes, she had painted all Dad's toenails in her favourite purple sparkly nail polish.

Feeling very pleased with herself, Lucy sat looking at the gleaming toes. They were much nicer purple and sparkly, she thought. She thought all toes should be sparkly

purple, even Dad's. And then, quite
suddenly, she thought that maybe Dad
wouldn't think so, and she was scared at
what she'd done. Downstairs she could hear
Mum and Will coming to the end of their
argument, and she began to panic. As
quickly and carefully as she could, she put
Dad's socks back on, and his shoes, and just
as she was finishing doing up the laces, Dad
woke with a grunt, saying, 'And the sulky-
minkey said . . . the silly-money . . . Oh.'

He sat on the edge of the bed, looking
baffled. 'I think I must have nodded off for
a few seconds,' he said at last. Lucy waited
anxiously for him to ask her what she'd
been doing while he was asleep, but he
didn't. He tucked her into bed, kissed her
goodnight, and went downstairs. A few
minutes later, Will came up to read on his
own, and he didn't ask her what she'd been
doing either. She lay in bed, thinking
nervously about what would happen when
Dad found out that his toes were purple and
sparkly. She felt very worried, but somehow

it didn't stop her being tired, and, before she knew it, she was asleep.

Next morning, Dad went off early to catch a train to London, so he wasn't at breakfast. By now he must have seen his toes, and Lucy wondered how cross he was. It was peculiar that Mum didn't say anything about it while they were having breakfast, but perhaps Dad wanted to tell Lucy off himself. Thinking that made her sad.

There wasn't much she could do about it, but she thought that if she was good all day Dad might forgive her a little bit, so she cleared the table for Mum and brushed her own hair, and at school she didn't get cross when Miss Petz spoke to her in her dark green voice, and when she came home from school she tidied her room without being asked. And to her surprise, her good behaviour worked so well that when Dad came home later in the evening he didn't say anything at all to her about his toes. Nothing.

'How are you feeling, Dad?' she asked
nervously.

'Still tired,' he said.

She waited for him to say something else,
but he didn't.

'It's time for bed,' Mum said. 'Will you
call Will, Poodle? He's in the street.'

Will came in from roller-blading with his hair dripping and his shirt all wet.

'Is it raining, Will?'

Will shrugged. 'Dunno.' He didn't usually notice things like that.

'But you're soaking.'

'Am I?'

Dad tutted. 'You're the most unobservant person I know, Will. You wouldn't notice if you found yourself under water. Now up you go.'

They went upstairs and got ready for bed, and Dad came up after them to read a story. He sat on the bed yawning.

'Why are you still tired?' Lucy asked.

'I've been working late every night,' he said. 'And I've been getting up early too. It's dark when I get into bed, and it's dark when I get dressed in the morning. It's terrible. Next week, I'm going to have a good rest.'

He began the story about the silk-monkey

again, but he couldn't keep his eyes open
and, for the second night running, he fell
asleep in the middle of reading it. Lucy sat
next to him, thinking. She thought carefully
about what Dad had said, testing it in her
mind to make sure she understood it. Then
she tried to think of a plan.

'Will,' she whispered at last.

Will grunted. He was balancing backwards on the edge of his bunk trying to
work out how Spiderman clung upside
down to ceilings. There was a crash.

'Will?' Lucy whispered again. 'Dad's
fallen asleep.'

Will nodded briefly and began to eye the
ceiling again.

'I need your help, Will.'

'What sort of help?'

'You have to ask Mum to borrow her
nail polish remover.'

'Have you got it
on the carpet again?'

'No. I just need to borrow it.'

'I'm busy. I have to practise on my ceiling.'

'I'll give you a choice from my sweet hoard.'

Without saying anything, Will climbed off the top bunk and went downstairs. Two minutes later, he came back up.

'She's run out,' he said. 'Where's your hoard?'

Lucy bit her lip to stop herself crying, but she bit it too hard.

Will peered at her face. 'Why are you crying?' he said. 'Don't you have any sweets in your hoard?'

Lucy put her fingers to her lips. Then she sat next to Dad's feet, and carefully, without waking him up, took off his shoes and socks.

Will gawped. 'Dad wears nail polish on his toes!' he exclaimed in a whisper. 'How did you find out? Who's going to tell Mum?'

Lucy explained.

'You're in big trouble,' Will said cheerfully. Lucy cried a bit more, and Will felt sorry for her. 'Don't worry,' he said. 'Perhaps it comes off with spit.'

But it didn't.

They sat looking at Dad's toes.

'I'm getting used to it,' Will said after a while. 'Perhaps he'll get used to it too.'

Lucy didn't think so. She went downstairs on her own to look through Dad's toolbox for removing things, and when she came back she found Will crouching over Dad's feet, giggling to himself.

'What are you doing?' she hissed.

'Nothing,' Will said, looking embarrassed. 'Not much.'

Lucy pushed him out of the way and saw that while she'd been downstairs he had put two of her best green and red Chinese dragon transfers round each of Dad's ankles. The effect was startling, like small animals dressed up in fashion clothes.

'You twit,' Lucy said. 'You pig twit. Red and green don't even go with purple.'

'I think they look good,' Will said stubbornly.

'Now we're both going to get into trouble,' Lucy said.

'What do you mean, "we"? You painted his nails. I was just trying to make it look more normal.'

'Four dragons isn't normal!'

Dad gave a low, sleepy grunt, and they both jumped.

'Quick! Put his shoes and socks back on.'

Dad began to mumble, 'And then the

sock-molley . . . the sick-milky . . . Oh.'
And he opened his eyes.

'Morning!' Will said. 'I'm just
straightening your shoelaces for you.'

After Dad had tucked them in and
staggered off, Will and Lucy lay awake
thinking sadly about how much trouble
they were going to get into. First they
bickered about who was going to get into

the most trouble, then, when they
were too tired to bicker any more,
they wondered together what they
were going to do.

'He'll see his feet as soon as he
goes to bed,' Will said gloomily.
'Probably we'll hear him shouting
and using bad language.'

But Lucy told him that Dad was working
so late he went to bed after Mum had
put the light out. 'Then he gets up
early in the morning when it's
still dark. That's why he didn't
notice yesterday.'

Will began to be hopeful.

'Perhaps we can just wait until the polish wears off.'

Lucy tried to feel hopeful too.

'In the meantime,' Will went on, 'we mustn't let him take his shoes and socks off during the day.'

Lucy agreed. 'Do you think we'll manage it, Will?' she asked.

'I think so,' Will said breezily. 'Who takes their shoes and socks off during the day?'

The next day was Saturday, and Dad decided to take them swimming at the leisure centre. Both Will and Lucy were very fond of swimming. They packed their costumes and towels in rucksacks and set off on their bikes.

Lucy was a safe cyclist and Dad was a boring cyclist, but Will was an exciting one. Skidding, swooping, swerving and cycling no-hands were his favourite tricks, and Dad was always telling him off.

'Watch out, Will!' Dad shouted.

'What?'

'You nearly collided with those people.'

'I didn't.'

'You did.'

'I didn't, I swerved to avoid them at the last second.'

'You shouldn't have been on the pavement in the first place. You really don't seem to notice what's going on around you.'

They reached the leisure centre, and paid their money, and went into the swimming pool area. It was a curvy pool with a sloping end like a beach, and a cafe, and hot showers, and a row of changing cubicles with clean white doors. Dad sat on his towel at the edge of the pool while Will and Lucy got into their costumes, and when they came out he said, 'I'm going to come in straightaway today.' He began to undo the laces of his shoes.

'No!' said Lucy suddenly, remembering the nail polish.

'Don't!' said Will, remembering the transfers.

'What's the matter with you two?' Dad said.

Will and Lucy looked desperately at each other for help. 'I was just wondering,' Will said, and hesitated.

Lucy said, 'Yes, I was too.'

'We were both just wondering,' Will

began again slowly, 'if it's a good idea to go swimming after all.'

'Of course it is,' Dad said impatiently. 'The water looks lovely and warm.'

'You don't always swim,' Lucy said. 'Sometimes you sit and chat instead.'

Dad looked round the pool. 'There's no one I know to chat to,' he said. 'Besides, I want to swim.'

'You could chat to *us*,' Will said. 'I'd like to chat.'

'About what?' Dad said, looking puzzled.

Will tried to think of something. Out of the corner of his eye, he saw Lucy making frantic signals. He shut his eyes and frowned so hard he thought he'd twisted his forehead, but nothing came to mind. 'I've forgotten,' he said at last in a weak voice.

'Ah well.' Dad took off one shoe.

'I remember now!' Will shouted.

'What?'

'Do you like eye-drops?'

This took Dad by surprise. One of the good things about Dad was that he could

be taken by surprise. 'Eye-drops? You mean, drops you put in your eyes?'

'Let's start by talking about that sort,' Will said. He fixed Dad with an alert stare. 'Do you like them?'

'I don't understand what you mean, Will, do I *like* them?' Dad made an exasperated noise. 'Nobody *likes* eye-drops. They just use them. I don't know why you want to talk about them, it's maddening. I'm going to get changed now.' He took hold of his sock.

'Anyway,' Will continued quickly, 'how much do eye-drops cost these days?'

'Listen,' Dad said crossly. 'I'm not getting into a conversation about eye-drops.'

Will looked cunning. 'What do you mean by "conversation"?' he asked.

Dad stared at Will. 'Are you all right?' he said. 'How much Coke

have you drunk today?'

'I'm not all right,' Lucy said suddenly.

'She's not,' Will said firmly. 'She's not all right at all.' Both he and Dad looked at Lucy.

One of the things Lucy was good at was making herself cry. No one was as good as her. She did it by thinking about sad things, like seal pups being killed and the time she caught her thumb in the car door.

She let her face go wide, and her eyes spilled over with tears.

'Poodle!' Dad murmured. 'Poodle-fish!' He got up and rocked her in a hug. 'What is it?'

That was quite a hard question. Lucy thought about it. 'It's about people not liking eye-drops,' she sobbed.

Dad straightened up. 'There's something going on here,' he said sternly. 'I don't know what it is, but I don't like it. We've come to the pool to swim. The water is lovely and warm. I'm going to swim.' He took hold of his sock again, and, without

25

thinking, Will leaped into the water and began to thrash and scream.

'It's freezing!' he yelled. 'It's freezing cold!'

He leaped out of the water and did a mad-frozen-person's dance on the side, watched by everyone in the pool.

A life-guard ran over. 'What's the problem?' he asked.

'He says the water's cold,' Dad explained. 'But I'm afraid he's insane. I'm sure it's fine.'

The life-guard looked shifty. 'Well,' he said. 'The heater did break down overnight, and it's a little chillier than usual.'

Dad looked worried. 'I don't like it cold,' he said.

'Freezing,' Will said. 'Honestly, I still can't feel my elbows. I'm going to get changed back into my clothes.'

Dad tested the water with his hand and looked doubtful.

Will was inspired. He said,

'Dad, I'm going to buy a drink with my pocket money. Why don't you have a coffee to warm yourself up after putting your hand in that freezing water? They sell papers at the cafe too. I saw a headline about that football game last night.'

Dad looked interested. 'It can't hurt to have a bit of a read first,' he said.

Will and Lucy were very pleased with themselves. That night, as they lay in bed, they bickered in a friendly way about who had been the most distracting person to Dad.

'I distracted him most,' Will said, 'with the conversation.'

Lucy said, 'I distracted him second most with crying.'

They lay there, thinking about this.

'It's funny about Dad, isn't it?' Will said after a while. 'He's all right. Then suddenly he gets shouty. Then he's all right again.'

'It *is* funny,' Lucy said. 'He makes me laugh.'

'He's all right, though,' Will said.

Lucy said, 'He *is* all right.'

'Do you think that nail polish has worn off by now?'

'Probably. But I bet the transfers are still there.'

Will lay there trying not to think of this. 'That's the problem with Dad,' he said at last. 'He changes his mind so much, and doesn't know what's going on, and falls asleep when he shouldn't.'

'Mum's not like that,' Lucy said.

'Mum always knows what's going on,' Will agreed.

'Mum wouldn't have been distracted by a conversation,' Lucy said.

'Or crying.'

'Mum would have seen her feet by now,' Lucy said. 'And she'd be cross,' she added.

Will sighed. 'That's the good thing about Dad,' he said. 'Luckily for us.'

'Do you think Dad will *ever* see his feet, Will?' Lucy asked.

Will thought for a minute. 'I don't think

so,' he said. 'He's too unobservant. He doesn't notice what's going on around him.'

And, thinking about that, they both fell asleep.

They were woken suddenly by shouting. Someone outside their room was groaning, and someone else was calling, 'What's going on? Are you all right?' And everything was confused.

It was dark, and Will and Lucy opened their eyes and looked into the blackness, and listened.

One of the voices was Mum's and one of them was Dad's. Mum's was the one shouting, 'Are you all right?' And Dad's was the one going, 'Aaah, ngh, oof.'

For a moment, Will and Lucy were

frightened. There were running footsteps on
the stairs, and their bedroom door was
pulled open. Mum stood there in the sudden
bright light wearing skinny pink pyjamas,
saying quickly, 'Dad's fallen down the
stairs!'

There was a lot of bustling about, and
questions being shouted, and Will and Lucy
putting on their dressing gowns in a big
rush, and Mum telling them not to be upset,
and Dad groaning. Everyone was pale and
tight-faced, especially Dad.

'What happened?' Will said.

'He was coming to bed in the dark,'
Mum said, 'and he missed the step and fell
downstairs. He's done something to his
foot.'

Dad lay on the stairs, nodding and groaning. Will went over and gave him a hug, and Lucy held his hand. Dad gave a bent and painful grin.

'He might have broken a toe,' Mum said. 'I know it's late, but we're all going to have to go to the hospital.'

Very slowly they helped Dad downstairs and into the car. Sometimes he pretended he was OK and didn't need help at all, and sometimes he did a jerky dance and roared with pain, and eventually they got him into the front passenger seat, and he lay there panting and smiling bravely.

It was strange driving through the streets in the middle of the night. Streetlights made quiet patterns over the road, and there was a washy sound different from the usual noise of traffic.

At the hospital they helped Dad to Accident and Emergency, and waited in the lounge until a doctor was available.

Dad kept wincing and grimacing.

'Don't worry, Dad,' Will said. 'It's only pain.'

'Not bad pain,' Lucy said comfortingly.

'It is bad, actually,' Dad said.

'Poor Dad,' Mum said. 'He's being very brave.' And Dad put on a brave look.

Will and Lucy weren't feeling tired any more. They were feeling worried and sad and somehow excited all at the same time. They had never been in a hospital at night before, and they sat in the lounge holding Dad's hands and looking round at everything.

A nurse came to talk to them, and went away again.

Half an hour later, Dad's name was called, and they helped Dad down a corridor and into a room where the doctor was waiting.

The doctor was a large smiling man with a hairy face, and to everyone's surprise he turned out to be one of Dad's friends. As soon as they realized this, they started laughing.

'This is Alan,' Dad said. 'We play football together every Thursday night.'

'Doesn't look like you'll be playing for a while,' Alan said. 'What happened? Sliding tackle? Overhead bicycle kick?'

'Fell down the stairs,' Dad said.

Alan nodded. 'That'll do it. Poor you. Well, we'd better have a look at it.'

Dad lay on a special bed, and Alan took off his shoe and looked at his stockinged foot. The big toe stuck out at a right angle.

'Almost certainly broken,' Alan said. 'I'm going to take your sock off now. It may hurt a bit.'

Dad nodded and gripped the sides of the bed.

Slowly Alan peeled off the sock, and
everyone stood quietly looking at Dad's
foot. Or not at his foot. At five purple
sparkly toes and two green and red Chinese
dragon transfers.

There was a moment of stunned silence. Alan raised his eyebrows, and Mum blinked and Dad's mouth fell open. And the children said together, 'I did that.'

Back at home the Quigleys sat in their kitchen drinking hot chocolate. It was four o'clock in the morning, and they felt very sleepy. Dad had a bulky white cast on his foot, and he sat with it up on a chair.

'No, I wasn't worried,' Mum was saying. 'If he'd been wearing nail polish for a long time I'd have noticed.'

Lucy was examining Dad's cast. 'Why did you choose white?' she asked. 'You could have chosen a different colour.'

'Like pink,' Will said. 'It would have gone with your toenails.'

Dad yawned. 'At least you both admitted doing it,' he said. 'It's not often you agree on anything.'

'Thank you,' Will said, yawning too. 'Even though it was really Lucy who did it,' he added.

'No, you did the tattoos,' Lucy said sleepily.

'The tattoos were just extra.'

'Dragon tattoos are never just extra.'

Even though they were so sleepy, they began to bicker. They bickered slowly between yawns all the way upstairs and into bed, and as they fell asleep they were still murmuring, 'You're going to get into trouble' and 'I don't think those dragons will ever wear off.'

Mum stood in the doorway watching them, and Dad stood looking at his foot.

'Do you really think the white cast doesn't go with the purple nail polish?' he asked anxiously.

'Don't worry,' Mum said. 'I've got lots of other colours you can choose from.'

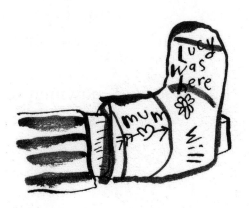

Lucy's Big Day

Lucy's Big Day

Lucy's birthday was coming up, and she was going to have a party. The Quigleys had a meeting about it in their back room.

'I don't know what sort of party I want,' Lucy said. 'But I want it to be perfect.' She only had one birthday a year so she thought this was fair.

'We want it to be perfect too,' Mum said.

'We do,' Dad said.

Only Will disagreed. He said, 'Perhaps it could go a bit wrong. That would be cool.' Will was in that sort of mood.

They began to talk about the party. It was hard choosing because Lucy wanted it to be different from all her friends' parties.

'What about a swimming party?' Mum asked.

'Inez had a swimming party.'

'Or a trip to the cinema?'

'Ellie went to the cinema.'

Mum and Dad suggested over twenty different sorts of party, including a pyjama party, a fancy-dress party, a sleepover party, a visit-to-a-museum party, a climbing-wall party, a funfair party, a trip-to-London party, a bowling party, a picnic party and a going-to-a-show-and-meeting-the-cast-for-tea-afterwards party, but Lucy's friends had done them all already.

'What about a luxury trip to EuroDisney just for the family?' Will suggested.

Dad and Will had an argument. Dad said Will was not taking things seriously, and Will said he was taking things very seriously, in fact more seriously than anyone else, otherwise why was he the only person suggesting expensive things, and Dad said he bet Lucy didn't think Will was

taking things seriously. And Lucy seriously
told them both to shut up.

Then they started again.

'All we have to do is think of
the perfect party,' Mum said.
'How hard can that be?'

They thought hard. Will
thought so hard he fell off
his chair, and was told to sit
still and not fidget, and for a
while it looked like Dad and
Will were going to have
another argument.

'What about this?' Mum
said at last. 'A traditional party at
home. With games like Pass the Parcel and
Musical Chairs, and dancing competitions,
and some magic, and a treasure hunt, and a
really wonderful tea with all your favourites
like chessboard sandwiches and cheese
straws and ice-cream clowns and ginger-
bread aliens and refrigerator cake. A traditional party is the one sort of party that
none of your friends have had.'

This sounded good. Perhaps not perfect, but definitely good. Lucy said she'd think about it, and the next day she said all right.

When Lucy's friends got their invitations, they thought it sounded good too. Perhaps not perfect, but definitely good. Most of them had never been to a traditional party before and were excited and confused at the same time. 'What happens at a traditional party?' they asked.

At home Lucy asked Mum to remind her what happened, and Mum described some of the games, like Make Them Laugh and the Memory Game. Will had agreed to do some magic, she said. 'And Dad's thinking up some extra surprises.'

'What sort of surprises?' Lucy asked suspiciously. 'I only want really good party surprises, I don't want ordinary surprises like Dad falling downstairs again.'

Mum said Dad was thinking of some really good party surprises.

That evening, after Will and Lucy had

gone to bed, Mum and Dad sat in the front room talking about the surprises.

'Lucy's worried,' Mum said. 'Are you sure this is going to work?'

Dad said he was sure. He said he'd found the right costumes and tried them on. It was true that in one of them he couldn't see, and the other made it hard for him to breathe. 'But they both fit,' he said. 'And that's the main thing.'

Upstairs in bed, Lucy and Will were talking about the party as well.

'What sort of magic are you going to do, Will?' Lucy asked.

Will didn't answer for a while. Then, in a strange, whiskery voice, he said, 'You know not who you ask. I am not Will. I am the Great Conjurina, Mage of the Land of Wigs and Novelties. Anyway, magicians never talk about their tricks,' he added.

'You have to talk to me, because it's my party,' Lucy said. 'What trick are you doing?'

'I thought I'd do the egg one.'

'Not the egg one, Will! You always break the egg.'

'I've been practising.'

Lucy lay in bed, trying hard not to think badly about her party. She had a horrible feeling it wasn't going to be perfect. It was a sad, anxious feeling, a bit like finishing a packet of sweets and realizing there are none left.

In the week before her party, Lucy often had the feeling. She told Mum about it.

'I can't stop thinking my party's going to go wrong.'

Mum said that all she needed to do was tell herself it was going to be fine, and her sad thoughts would disappear. But Mum must have made a mistake because although Lucy repeated to herself six times every bedtime that her party was going to be perfect, when she woke in the morning she still had the anxious feeling in her tummy.

Sometimes she had an even worse thought. She told Dad about it.

'What happens if my feeling *makes* the party go wrong?'

But Dad just looked at her funny.

As soon as she woke on the morning of her party, Lucy could feel it in her tummy, the anxious feeling. It hadn't gone away. In fact, it had got worse, and now it was a bit like feeling sick. No one else seemed to care. Mainly Mum and Dad were too busy, they kept going secretly into other rooms, where she heard them laughing and whispering to each other. When they spoke to her, they simply told her everything was going well.

'See for yourself. It's a lovely day. All the balloons are up, the refrigerator cake's turned out well. Even Will looks smart. Sort of.'

But Lucy's feeling made her see different things. Usually she wouldn't have noticed that her pink party tights were wrinkly from the wash, or the decorations in the front room weren't straight, or her party shoes were scuffed at the toes. Today, she noticed.

She went to find Dad, who was in the kitchen washing cake dough off his elbows. Will came in wearing a large silky moustache made the night before from a goatskin purse. He got half a dozen eggs from the fridge, grinned, dropped an egg on the floor, and left without clearing it up.

Lucy looked so sad that Dad stopped picking bits of cake off the window and

tried to comfort her. He said it was normal
to feel anxious about parties.

'Everyone feels anxious. But really,
everything's going to turn out fine.'

Lucy knew this was wrong, though. Lots
of things don't turn out fine. She left Dad
and went to find Mum.

Mum tried to comfort her. She admitted
that sometimes things go wrong, but said
that things can go right too, if you give
them a chance.

'How do you give them a chance?' Lucy
asked.

Mum said, 'By not getting cross with them straightaway. Do you know what I mean? Sometimes things don't go right at first but, if you give them a chance, they go right in the end.'

Lucy thought about this. 'Rubbish,' she said at last.

And Lucy was proved right almost at once, because when Mum helped her get changed into her party clothes, things that went wrong at first carried on going wrong afterwards. For instance, at first Lucy's tights were all wrinkly ('don't worry, the wrinkles will soon come out'), and then they itched ('never mind, the itching will soon stop'), and after that they kept slipping down ('yes, but they don't slip down *much*'). It was the same with her skirt. There was a stain on it to begin with, and after Mum had cleaned it there was a wet patch.

It didn't get any better when Dad did her hair. For some reason it was always Dad's job to do Lucy's hair. He did it every morning. He could do bunches, plaits and messy pony-tails. But he couldn't do French plaits, which is what Lucy wanted for her birthday party.

'That's not a French plait,' Lucy said after half an hour.

'It nearly is,' Dad said, examining it. 'It's a French splat.'

It was typical of Mum and Dad that they kept telling her things were fine when she could see they weren't. By the time her friends were due to arrive, Lucy was very sad. She stood in the hall on her own, waiting for the first knock on the door, and feeling a bit sick. If Mum and Dad were right, this was the moment when everything turned out fine. She crossed her fingers and had a go at crossing her toes.

Inez and Mary called Moo were the first to arrive, and Moo was wearing exactly the same skirt as Lucy, only without a wet patch. Ellie arrived, and Lottie, and Freya with her little sister, Grubby Gabby. Gilly came with Emmy, and Megan came with Sonya, and Charlotte came on her own. Everyone had brought a present for Lucy and by now she had nine identical sets of scented gel pens. A lot more people arrived in a clump, and they all crowded into the front room, where the party was going to begin with a story read by Mum.

'What's the story about?' Inez asked.

'It's called *Dotty Comes to the Party*,' Mum said, positioning herself on the sofa with some sheets of paper. 'Is everyone here now?'

'Pokehead and Tim aren't.'

'We'll wait then.'

Lucy didn't want to wait. Having to wait seemed too much like things going wrong. But Mum said she had to be patient.

'Don't worry,' Mum said. 'It won't spoil anything. They'll be here any second.'

Meanwhile, crouching behind the sofa in a full-length Dalmatian dog outfit, Dad shifted weight and groaned to himself. He hadn't realized there would be so little room. He was doubled-up, with the large blunt snout of his enormous dog-head crushed against his black-spotted legs. He was very hot. The dog costume was made of thick fake fur and smelled of the hundreds of other Dads who had worn it before him.

The plan was this. Mum would read a story about Dotty the Dalmatian coming to Lucy's party, and when it got to the bit where Dotty arrived, Dad would leap out surprisingly from behind the sofa with a bag

of Mars Bars. Waiting patiently for his cue, he heard Mum say that she would wait for Pokehead and Tim, and groaned again. He thought if they didn't come soon he would have lost the use of his legs.

Twenty minutes later, all the children were bored and fidgety. Everyone kept asking Lucy why the party hadn't started, even though they all knew. Lucy kept asking Mum why Dad couldn't play some games with them, and Mum kept saying Dad was busy. Even after Tim and Pokehead arrived there was a delay while they argued about who had lost the scented gel pens which they had meant to bring as a present.

'It doesn't matter!' Lucy said crossly. 'I just want the party to start now!'

At last, Mum began to read. In the story, Dotty the Dalmatian was trying to get to Lucy's party, but he was lost. He bumped into strange people, who gave him directions, but he kept getting things wrong, and the children had to shout out when he

made mistakes. In the story it took him a
long time to get to the right street, and,
after that, a long time to get to the right
house.

'But finally,' Mum said, 'he made it. And
there was a knock on the door.' Here, to
everyone's surprise, there was a real knock,
which sounded as if it came from behind the
sofa. All the children in the room fell silent.

'And then,' Mum said dramatically,
'Dotty appeared!'

Nothing happened.

Mum said again, a bit louder, 'Dotty
appeared!'

Without warning, a misshapen creature
with an over-large head lurched from
behind the sofa with a bellow of
pain, and staggered forward making a noise like someone eating
something revolting. There was
general uproar in the Quigleys'
front room, with children
screaming and running to hide
and falling over. Mary called

Moo was knocked to the ground, Pokehead
spat her chewing gum the length of the room,
and Grubby Gabby wet herself in terror. No
one quite knew what was happening until
at last the creature pulled off its own head,
and Dad stood there, sweating and saying
sorry and grimacing with pain.

Even Lucy hadn't expected things to go
wrong this badly. For half an hour the
party was totally forgotten while Grubby
Gabby was taken home and Moo treated
for bruising where she'd been trampled by
other children.

Lucy went to talk to Dad.

'I knew it would go wrong,' she said.

'And now it has.'

Dad looked crestfallen. He began to explain about being in pain.

'You didn't even remember the Mars Bars,' she said.

Dad looked more crestfallen. 'I'm sorry. But look at it this way, Poodle. At least it can't get any worse. The party's bound to get better now.'

It didn't.

Although nothing else went spectacularly wrong, lots of little things didn't go as they should. At Musical Chairs, Lucy was first person out when her hair fell into her eyes and she sat on Will instead of a chair. In Pass the Parcel, the main prize was won by Charlotte by mistake. In the dancing competition, Pokehead had to be disqualified for bad behaviour, and Lucy's tights started coming down so she had to give up. Other people seemed to be enjoying themselves, though Ellie told her that the prizes had been better at Sonya's party, and Pokehead said that she didn't think the Spotty Monster had been as scary as everyone else seemed to think.

By now, Lucy couldn't think of anything except how bad her party was. She got sadder and sadder.

She stopped trying to smile.

She stopped talking to her friends.

And when the Great Conjurina took the stage and solemnly smashed seven eggs one

after the other, she went upstairs alone to
her room and shut the door.

Whenever Lucy was very sad, she got
into the narrow space between the bed and
the wall and covered herself with the
blanket from her doll's pram, and tried to
think of not being Lucy. Squeezing her eyes
shut, she began to cry big, angry tears.

After a while there was a knock on the
bedroom door.

'Lucy?'

She stayed where she was.

'Lucy?'

When she lifted her blanket, Mum and Dad and Will were standing by the door.

'I know what you're going to say,' Lucy said, between sobs. 'And I'm not listening. Everything's gone wrong, and it's not all going to turn out fine. It's the worst party ever.'

There was a small silence, and Mum said, 'You're right. It is.'

Lucy didn't hear her because she was already saying, 'And the worst thing of all is the feeling. First it was like no more sweets, and then it was like going to be sick and now it's like people poking me and not being able to stop them. What did you say?' she said.

'I agree with you. It's the worst party ever. There's no point in pretending otherwise.'

Dad agreed too. 'And the worst bit was Dotty the Disgusting Dalmatian,' he said. 'I thought he'd actually killed Grubby Gabby. Think of that, a party where a small girl is crushed to death by an over-

sized cartoon dog.'

'The other worst bit,' Will said, 'was the egg trick. It was really terrible, especially the egg that ended up on the light-shade. And the one that squirted into Tim's orange squash wasn't any better.'

Lucy came out from behind the bed. 'Getting about a hundred scented gel pens and nothing else was another worst bit,' she said. 'And not winning Pass the Parcel.'

'And what about Moo getting trampled?' Mum said.

'And Pokehead thinking that wrestling move counted as dancing,' Will said. 'She could have broken Tim's neck.'

'And Lucy's tights falling round her ankles in the middle of her *Saturday Night Fever* routine,' Dad said. 'It's all been terrible.'

Lucy said, a bit proudly, 'This is the worst party I've ever had.'

And Will said, 'I expect it's the worst party in the history of the world. Probably it'll be famous.'

They all grinned, even Lucy. 'I don't know why, but my feeling's not so bad any more,' she said shyly.

Mum got organized again. 'Right. What shall we do with the rest of this rubbish party?' she said. 'All that's left is the treasure hunt and tea. But we can skip them, if you want to.'

Lucy shook her head. 'It's OK.'

'What if they go wrong?'

'It won't make any difference now.'

And so the Quigleys hurried back down to the last bit of the awful party.

First it was the treasure hunt. Clues had been hidden all over the house and garden on bits of paper, saying things like: *Lift the laun-*

61

dry basket's lid, *To find out where the next clue's hid.*

And: *Find some pansies in a pot, Feel underneath to find the spot.*

Everyone began to rush from one clue to the next, trying to be the first to reach the hidden treasure.

Meanwhile, in the kitchen, Dad changed into his second costume of the day, a pirate's outfit.

'I wasn't going to do it after the bog-up with the dog,' he said to Mum. 'But Lucy's feeling happier now. Anyway, I'm going to keep it very simple. I'm not going to bother with the hook or the parrot or the fake scar.' He put on an eye patch, a fluffy beard and a striped head-scarf, and said, 'What do you think? I don't look scary, do I? They'll all be able to recognize me, won't they? I'm just Beardy Bob, the friendly pirate dishing out the treasure.'

But Mum was distracted. 'What's that smell?' she said, sniffing.

They both sniffed.

Dad opened the freezer door, and dirty water flooded onto the floor. There was a sudden foul smell of rotten meat.

'Wonderful,' Dad said. 'Now the freezer's packed up.'

'Lucy was right,' Mum said. 'Everything's going wrong today. Quick, empty the freezer while I finish laying out the tea.' She looked at her watch. 'You've got about five minutes before they reach the treasure.'

As fast as he could, Dad began to haul things out of the freezer: bloody lamb chops, sticky pieces of liver and limp steaks dripping with greasy juice. In his haste, his head-scarf fell off, but he fished it out of the flooded cabinet and jammed it back on his head.

'Quick!' Mum shouted from the other room. 'They're on their way!'

Wiping his hands on his beard and flipping his eye-patch back down, Dad bounded up the stairs to the loft, where he dragged a wooden chest from under the bed and arranged himself on it, panting slightly

63

and mopping his brow, listening to the thumping feet of children on the steps below.

Against all the odds, it had been a very good treasure hunt. Will and Tim, working together, had found most of the early clues first. Then Ellie and Inez were in the lead, finding five clues in quick succession.

Finally, totally by accident, Pokehead found the last clue: *To reach the treasure don't be soft, Just climb the stairs to a place aloft,* and, barging Tim out of the way, she led the race up the stairs to the attic room. Now all the children were together. They ran in a hot tangle up the top flight of steps, and burst chattering into the loft, where they stood rooted to the spot, totally silent.

A strange man they had never seen before sat on a wooden box glaring at them. He looked like a tramp, and stank like one too. His face and arms were smeared with something sticky, and red gloop hung from his beard.

'Ha-har,' he said suddenly, and the children skittered backwards. 'Now, now. No need to be timid,' he said in a strange, rough voice. 'You know old Beardy Bob, don't 'ee?'

The children shook their heads. This seemed to surprise Beardy Bob. He leaned down to Lucy and hissed something quietly. It sounded like, 'It's me, you idiot, can't you see?' Then he went on in his old booming voice. 'Well, you might not know me, but I knows you.' He fixed his one good eye on Pokehead. 'I recollect your face,' he growled. 'What be your name?'

'Pokehead,' Pokehead said shyly.

'Pokehead?' the man shouted, and the children skittered backwards again. 'Didn't I

sail with 'ee on the *Black Terror* back in
ninety-nine?'

Pokehead shook her head quickly. 'No,
sir. Wasn't me, sir.'

The man scratched his beard. 'Must have
been some other Pokehead,' he muttered.
'Now then, whose house be this I've washed
up in?'

Lucy put her hand up, and the man
stared at her. Will went and stood next to
her and held her hand, and together they
looked back at the dirty stranger.

'Will,' Lucy whispered. 'Do you think
Mum and Dad know he's here?'

The stranger let out an odd laugh which
he immediately swallowed. 'Do they know?
They know all right, young missy. It be
they who asked me to come here with my
chest of treasure. And here it be. You be the
birthday girl, young missy, and this be your
treasure!' He got up and limped all round it
and flung open the lid. It was full to the
brim with sweets and chocolates and Mars
Bars. This made a big difference. As soon as

they saw what was in the chest, the children got over their shock. Beardy Bob seemed friendlier once he was handing out sweets, though none of them dared go too close to him, and he didn't smell any better.

'That's real blood, you know,' Pokehead whispered to Lucy.

Beardy Bob paused in handing out sweets. 'Blood?' he said, surprised. He wiped his face and beard, and looked at his hand. 'Yuck,' he said with disgust.

'It is real, isn't it?' Pokehead asked.

Beardy Bob recovered. 'A course it be real,' he growled. He chuckled dangerously. ''Tis the pure clean blood of an innocent child.' He winked at Lucy.

Lucy stared at him, baffled.

'Wink, wink,' Beardy Bob said helpfully. He pulled down his beard briefly and grinned. He was a very strange man with a terribly stained face, but he wasn't scary any more.

One by one, the children got their sweets and went downstairs. Beardy Bob seemed very keen that Lucy, who hadn't actually won the treasure hunt, should have as many sweets as possible. 'Are you sure you can't be carrying more?' he asked.

Lucy shook her head. 'Don't worry,' she said kindly as she left. 'You see, today's a day when everything goes wrong, and it doesn't really matter.'

Over the next few weeks at school, Lucy's friends often talked about the party. But the odd thing was that no one thought it had

been the slightest bit awful.

'But what about Dotty the Dalmatian?' Lucy said.

They thought Dotty had been the most wonderfully shocking thing they had ever seen. They liked all the games, and all the food, and Charlotte said she had never won a prize at a birthday party before, and she would remember it for the rest of her life.

But best of all had been Beardy Bob. Pokehead told everyone in a hushed voice that Lucy had had a real pirate 'with real blood', and soon Lucy's party had become famous for being good.

Only the Quigleys disagreed. When they talked about the party at home, they enjoyed reminding themselves how everything had gone wrong.

'It's very odd,' Lucy said at last. 'Talking to my friends, and then talking to you, it's hard to know whether it was the best worst party ever, or the worst best party ever. But I agree with Charlotte. I don't suppose I'll ever forget it.'

Will's Big Effort

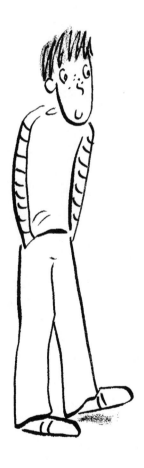

Will's Big Effort

The Quigleys went away for the weekend and they took with them a boy they didn't know called Robinson Potts.

'Why are we taking him?' Will and Lucy asked.

Mum explained that Robinson Potts was the son of an old friend of hers, who had just come back to the city after living away.

'And now she's got the flu,' Mum said. 'I told her we could take Robinson with us this weekend, and it would give her a rest.'

Will and Lucy wanted to know more about Robinson Potts.

'He's the same age as Will, I think.'

'Is he nice?' Lucy asked.

'I'm sure he is.'

'Does he like skateboarding?' Will asked.

'I've no idea.'

'Or surfing, or paragliding, or bungee-jumping?'

'Will, you've never done any of those things yourself.'

Lucy put her hand up. 'Will he be interested in collecting seaweed?'

Mum said that she didn't know what Robinson Potts was interested in, she only knew that his mum had flu and needed a break. 'It's just for the weekend,' she said. 'Anyway, I think it'll be fun to have someone new with us, don't you?'

Will and Lucy said they didn't know. Mum asked Dad, and Dad said straight-away he thought it would be fun, but he looked as if he hadn't been listening.

On Friday afternoon, the Quigleys packed the car and went to pick up Robinson Potts. When they got to his house, they found him waiting at the gate with his bags.

Will and Lucy examined him through the car window. He was a small, wide boy with bushy black hair and a round face that

didn't move much. He looked back at them
through the window.

'Do you like him yet?' Lucy whispered.

'I don't know,' Will whispered back.

Mum got out of the car to say hello.

'You're seven minutes late,' Robinson
Potts said. He kept looking at his watch.
'Eight minutes,' he said after a moment.

Mum looked taken aback by this, but she
said she was sorry and went inside to talk to
Robinson Potts's mum.

Dad took over. After he had said hello
and put Robinson Potts's bags in the boot,
he told Will and Lucy to make room for

him on the back seat.

'I usually sit in the front,' Robinson Potts said in a flat voice.

Dad explained that it was against the law for children to ride in the front on motorways. Robinson Potts stared at him sulkily without saying anything, then slowly got into the back.

Will and Lucy had been reminded before-hand to introduce themselves, but when Will said, 'Hello, I'm Will,' Robinson Potts just said, 'I know,' and when Lucy introduced herself, he didn't say anything at all. He sat there breathing heavily and looking out of the window until they set off.

Robinson Potts was a boy who didn't say much. He didn't say much when Mum and Dad asked him about his new house, and he didn't say anything to Lucy when she gave him a detailed description of the Quigleys' own house. Occasionally Mum said cheerful things to him like, 'I'm so glad you're coming with us, we'll be able to show you the Valley of the Rocks,' but he just shrugged. And in the middle of Dad explaining the things they could do at the weekend, such as rock-pooling and beach-games, he got out his GameBoy and started to play on it.

He wasn't just uncommunicative. He was hard to be with. After a while, Dad put on a CD, and Robinson Potts said that loud music made him feel ill, and Dad turned it off. To cheer everyone up, Mum passed round a tin of travel sweets. They all liked travel sweets, especially Lucy.

'Please can I have the purple one?' she asked. 'Please! There's only one left, and they're my favourite.'

'Offer them to Robinson first,' Mum said. 'He's our guest.'

Robinson Potts took the purple one.

They drove the rest of the way in silence.

It was eight o'clock in the evening when they arrived. Dad parked the car in front of the cottage, and they got out and stretched, and began to feel in a holiday mood. At the bottom of the hill they could see a bit of sea, grey and glittering. The air smelled different, as if the sky were somehow bigger or looser, and all the birds had strange, excited voices.

When they had unpacked the car they had a special late tea, which they had brought with them: cold chicken and salad, one of their favourites.

Robinson Potts said that he didn't like chicken.

'Just eat what you can,' Mum said kindly.

'I'm allergic,' he said. 'I can't eat it and I can't go near it either.'

'How about some salad then?' Dad said.

Robinson Potts put on a disgusted expression. 'I don't eat *salad*. I've never eaten *salad*. Anyway, I'm not hungry.' Without asking, he left the table and went and sat on the sofa.

The Quigleys ate tea on their own. 'By the way,' Will said. 'I'm not so bothered about salad either.' But nobody seemed to hear him.

For pudding there were apple turnovers or ice-cream, and Robinson Potts's appetite recovered enough for him to eat three turnovers very fast, one after the other. After he'd finished them, he asked what flavour the ice-cream was.

'Salad,' Will said, and got told off.

At bedtime, while Robinson Potts was brushing his teeth, Will went to talk to Mum. 'It's about Robinson Potts,' he said.

'What about him?'

Will wondered how to say it. He didn't want to seem rude, so he tried to think of the words Mum used when she told him off. It was hard to choose the right one because there were quite a few of them. 'He's . . . difficult,' he said at last.

Mum nodded, and Will was encouraged.

'And selfish,' he added. He thought a bit more. 'And unhelpful,' he went on. 'And uncommunicative. And untruthful. And obstructive. And inconsiderate.' He stopped, fearing Mum was going to be cross with him.

'You're right,' Mum said. 'He is.'

Will breathed a sigh of relief. 'Good,' he said. 'I just wanted to check I didn't have to be nice to him.'

'Unfortunately you do,' Mum said. 'He's our guest.'

Will was amazed. 'I didn't invite him.'

'It doesn't matter, he's still our guest. You have to make a big effort to be nice to him.'

Will was more amazed.

Mum said, 'Listen, Will. I don't know why he's difficult and selfish and all those other things. But we have to be nice to him anyway. Perhaps he's shy. Try to talk to him a bit more. Get to know him.'

'It's hard to talk to someone who doesn't say anything back.'

'If you're nice to him, he'll be nice to you. Now, promise me you'll make a big effort.'

Reluctantly Will promised, and went back to the room he was sharing with Robinson Potts.

It was late by now. Dad read the boys a story, and said goodnight and switched the light off.

Immediately, Robinson Potts reached over and turned the bedside light back on. 'I always have the light on,' he said.

Dad looked distracted. 'Will,' he said. 'Do you think you can get to sleep with the light on?'

Will opened his mouth, changed his mind, and shut it again. 'I suppose I can try,' he said, with a big effort. Dad looked pleased, and said goodnight, and left him with Robinson Potts.

For a while Robinson Potts sat up in bed playing on his GameBoy, and Will tried to

get to sleep. But the light and the bleeps
kept him awake. Eventually he sat up.
Remembering what Mum had said, he
thought he would try to get to know
Robinson Potts.

He cleared his throat and said the first
thing that came into his head. 'Done much
paragliding, Robinson?'

Robinson Potts didn't say anything.
Sitting in bed with his striped pyjamas
buttoned up to his chin, concentrating
frowningly on his GameBoy, he didn't look
like the sort of boy to have done any
paragliding at all.

Will sighed. 'Haven't done much paragliding myself,' he said. 'Or bungee-jumping. Or surfing. But you can surf down here, I've seen them. One day I'm going to have a go. I think I'd be pretty good at it. I'm a pretty determined person, Mum and Dad are always telling me I am. They don't use that word, they use another word. Stubborn. But they mean the same thing.'

Robinson Potts spoke. Without taking his eyes off his GameBoy, he said, 'I surf.'

Will stared at him. 'Really?'

'I could surf before I could walk. Surfing's nothing to me.'

Will stared some more.

'My uncle owns the best surf shop in Devon,' Robinson Potts added.

Will got excited. 'Where?'

Robinson Potts shifted uneasily in bed. 'Down the coast. I forget where.'

Will continued to be excited, so excited he found himself standing on his bed. 'We could ask to go surfing together tomorrow,' he said. 'If you say you want to surf too, I

bet Mum and Dad will let us. We can hire
wetsuits and boards, and swim out, and . . .'

'I don't surf any more,' Robinson Potts
said. 'Surfing's silly.' And, without saying
anything else, he went back to his
GameBoy.

Will got into bed again and pulled the
covers over his face. The bedside light
glowed through his sheet, and Robinson
Potts's GameBoy went *bleep, bleep,* and he
lay there for what seemed like hours, feeling
sad and confused, as he waited to fall asleep.

The first thing Will heard when he
woke next morning was the
bleeping of Robinson Potts's
GameBoy.

'Have you been doing that all
night?' he asked, yawning and
rubbing his eyes.

'I always wake early,'
Robinson Potts said. 'I've been
awake for hours while you've been asleep.
Snoring,' he added.

As he got dressed, Will thought hard about Robinson Potts. Mum had told him that thinking hard about difficult things made them easier to understand, but he had often noticed that this was totally untrue. Thinking hard about Robinson Potts made him feel slightly sick, like some maths problems did. He couldn't work out how to make Robinson Potts nice to him, it was as bad as 14 x 56 ÷ 8.

At breakfast, they all talked about what they were going to do that day. Everyone had a vote. Both Mum and Dad wanted to go for a walk, but Robinson Potts said that he had a loose ankle-bone, and the doctors had told him he mustn't walk far or his foot would fall off. Lucy wanted to play on the beach, but Robinson Potts said that sand gave him a rash. Will mentioned surfing, and looked at Robinson Potts hopefully, but when Robinson Potts didn't say anything, he said he wouldn't mind rock-pooling instead, and Robinson Potts said at once that rock-pooling was both boring and dangerous.

'What do you want to do, Robinson?' Dad asked, a little icily.

He shrugged.

'There must be something you'd like to do.'

'What *is* there to do in a place like this?'

The Quigleys all began to suggest things. Swimming, horse-riding, crazy golf or tennis, crab-bing, visiting a wildlife park, going to the arcade, cycling, taking a boat trip, fishing, going to the funfair, sightseeing, shopping for souvenirs, going to a museum.

Robinson Potts wasn't keen on any of them.

Dad said, rather impatiently, that they had to do something, and Robinson Potts reluctantly said he supposed that cycling wouldn't be too bad.

Lucy said, 'But we cycle every day to school. That's so boring!'

Immediately, Robinson Potts said that cycling was absolutely the only thing he wanted to do, but if nobody else wanted to do it he didn't mind going back to bed and playing on his GameBoy.

After he had gone back to his room, the Quigleys sat look-ing at each other. Dad got to his feet and began to walk up and down in a distracted way.

'That boy is spoiling everything,' he said crossly. 'I don't like him. He's selfish and unhelpful.'

'Not to mention "inconsiderate",' Will said.

'And "obstructive", "untruthful" and "uncommunicative",' Mum added.

'And horrid and sulky and a pig,' Lucy said, so as not to feel left out.

'Be quiet, Lucy,' Will said. 'You don't know the proper words.'

'They sound like good words to me,' Dad said grimly.

Mum calmed him down. 'Remember he's our guest,' she said. 'I've told Will he has to make a big effort, and so do you. I don't want you flying into a fit.'

Dad sighed. 'All right. We've got to think hard about what to do.'

'You can try,' Will said bitterly. 'But you'll find it's just like maths.'

For a few minutes, the Quigleys sat there thinking. Will came up with a plan involving deadly salad.

Suddenly Mum jumped up. 'I've got an idea,' she said. She went out into the hall and began to make telephone calls.

'What's Mum doing, Dad?' Lucy asked.

'I don't know, Poodle. I hope she's saving our holiday.'

Mum came back in. 'Guess what?' she said.

'You've just phoned Robinson Potts's mum to come and take him home?' Will said, his face brightening.

Mum shook her head. 'I've found a cycle trail that goes along a beach.'

'So?'

Dad grinned. 'Don't you see? We can cycle for a bit, which is what Robinson wants, then stop on the beach for games, which is what Lucy wants, then cycle for a bit more, then do some rock-pooling, which is what you want.'

Mum said, 'So we'll all be happy and cheerful and polite and pleasant.'

Will snorted. 'As if that's going to work,' he said.

At midday the Quigleys were spinning along the Tarka Trail cycle path. The trail ran along an estuary, on the route of a disused railway line. On one side there were marshes famous for bird-life and on the other there were dunes and beaches and the water. Every so often there was a bridge across one of the muddy streams flowing inland. There were other cyclists on the trail too. Some of them nodded or waved as they came past. And nearly all of them stared at Robinson Potts.

They stared at him because he was wearing his pyjamas. The top was buttoned up to his chin and the bottoms were tucked into his boots, and he looked like someone escaping from hospital.

When Dad had told him that they were going cycling after all, Robinson Potts had suddenly lost all enthusiasm for the idea. Long after Will was dressed, he was still sitting in bed playing on his GameBoy. Dad had to keep reminding him to get dressed. Eventually Dad got fed up. 'Listen, Robinson,' he said. 'We're running late. Next time I come into this room I want to see you out of those pyjamas.'

Five minutes later, Dad went back into the room and found Robinson Potts dressed in another pair of pyjamas.

'Robinson,' he said. 'You've misunderstood

 me. I want you out of all your pyjamas. I want you dressed in proper clothes so that we can go out.'

'These aren't pyjamas,' Robinson Potts said in his flat voice. 'They just look like pyjamas.'

But there was no time to argue, so Robinson Potts went cycling in his yellow and green striped pyjamas.

To begin with, they cycled for about five miles, pausing every so often to spot a bird in the marshes or take a drink from their water bottles. Robinson Potts didn't always pause when they did; he kept going, and they usually had to cycle hard to catch up with him again. At other times he stopped while they were still cycling, and they had to go back to find him. He rode in a powerful, slow style, hunched over the handlebars, staring at the ground and humming to himself.

At lunchtime, the Quigleys had a picnic and played French cricket on the beach. Robinson didn't play, because of the rash that was about to appear all over his body, but he told Will how he was holding the bat wrong, and, after a big effort, Will didn't argue.

Afterwards, they rock-pooled, and Will caught a blenny, which Robinson Potts identified as a 'madpole'. He knew every-thing about marine life, he said, and, after another big effort, Will said nothing.

Robinson Potts's pyjamas were very dusty by now, and ragged round the trouser bottoms where they had come out of his boots. One leg was completely damp where he had slipped into a rock pool. He looked very odd.

After rock-pooling, the time had come to turn round and head back to the car. They were all tired by now, and went slowly, with many rests. Robinson Potts, in his dusty, wet pyjamas, was in a bad mood, and cycled more slowly than ever,

complaining about his bike, other bikes, the
cycle track and the fact that no one had
told him what sort of clothes he would need
to wear.

When they were about halfway back, the
chain on Mum's bike came off. The children
didn't realize until Dad caught up with
them.

'I'll have to go back and help her,' he
said. 'You'd better wait for me here. You
can sit on that bench, if you like. But

whatever you do, don't go on the mud.'
Then he cycled away and soon disappeared
behind a hedge.

The children got off their bikes and sat
on the bench. Below them was a thin trickle
of water running through a great expanse
of mud. There was more mud than they
had ever seen before, flat and grey, covered
here and there with multi-coloured puddles
and old rubbish. An evil smell came off it.

Robinson Potts said he hated waiting for
people, and Will said nothing, and Lucy
said she quite enjoyed it and reminded
Robinson Potts how many times they had
waited for him.

Robinson Potts got to his feet. 'I'm going down,' he said.

'You're not allowed on the mud,' Lucy said.

'You're not,' Will added. 'Remember what Dad said.'

'He's not *my* dad,' Robinson Potts said. Leaving the bench, he walked down to the edge of the creek and began to fool around. First, he threw some small stones into the mud, to watch it splish up. Then he heaved in some bigger stones, and the mud spurted up in lumps. Finally, he dropped in an old house brick, and a thick flap of mud shot up his pyjama legs.

Lucy whispered, 'He's an idiot, isn't he, Will? I'm not wrong, am I?'

'You're not wrong.'

Lucy said, 'Quite a lot of the time I hate him. But other times he makes me want to laugh at him. Which is quite sad really.'

Will, who was tired of making so many big efforts to be nice to Robinson Potts, said he just hated him.

'What's he going to do now?'

Will shook his head. 'I just don't know,'
he said. 'But whatever it is I know I'm
going to have to make a big effort because
of it. And I'm fed up of making big efforts.'

Robinson Potts turned to stare at them.
'There's something stuck out there,' he
called. 'Out there in the mud.'

Will and Lucy looked. 'I can't see
anything,' Will called back.

Robinson Potts ignored him. He started to
hunt around the creek, picking up things
and taking them to the edge of the mud.

'What are you doing?' Lucy called.

'Something you couldn't do,' Robinson Potts said. Slowly he made a pile of the things he had found: some bits of plank, a cardboard box, an old tin tray, a few small logs. Taking careful aim, he threw one of the planks a little way into the mud, then, slightly further out, the tin tray, then, a bit further still, the cardboard box. He was making a sort of stepping-stone path across the mud.

'Oh no,' Will said.

Robinson Potts made a lumbering jump and landed on the plank, which immediately sank beneath him. Waving his arms wildly, he slithered from the plank onto the tin tray, which skidded sideways. Completely off-balance, he made a desperate lunge towards the cardboard box, missed it, and with a loud sucking plop sank up to his ankles in the mud.

Will and Lucy looked at each other.

'Here it comes,' Will said. 'The big effort.'

Robinson Potts stared at them from the mud. 'I'm not stuck, if that's what you think!' he shouted.

They watched him as he tried to get his feet out. At last he stopped trying, and stood there, wobbling gently.

'I am stuck!' he shouted. 'Don't just sit there. Help me.'

But Will had finally had enough of Robinson Potts. 'Why should I?' he shouted back.

That seemed to take Robinson Potts by surprise. He swayed to and fro in silence, thinking about it.

'Because you're my friend,' he cried out suddenly.

This took Will by surprise. He checked with Lucy. 'I'm not his friend, am I?' he asked.

Lucy thought about it. 'Perhaps you will be if you rescue him,' she said.

Will was very doubtful. He thought hard, and shouted to Robinson Potts, 'You're wrong. I'm not your friend. You've been horrible all weekend. Not just horrible, but difficult, unhelpful, inconsiderate, untruthful, obstructive and uncommunicative.'

Lucy said to Will, 'By the way, did you know that they're all the things Mum calls you?'

'Be quiet, Lucy. I'm not your friend, Robinson, and if I rescue you anyway it's only because I promised I'd make a big effort.'

Then Will went down to the mud. He took off his shoes and socks and rolled up his trouser legs, and waded out to Robinson Potts, and tugged him until he came unstuck, and helped him back to the shore. And waded out again with a bit of plank and dug out Robinson Potts's left shoe, which had got stuck in the mud, and brought it back. And went back to Lucy, who said, 'I'd hold your hand if it wasn't so muddy.' She helped Will clean his feet and legs with scratchy grass, and then they sat together by their bicycles, feeling fed up.

Robinson Potts sat on the bench. His

pyjamas were filthy and wet, and part of a
trouser leg had disintegrated. His face was
streaked with tears and there was mud in
his hair. Will and Lucy thought he was the
most miserable-looking, oddest person they
had ever seen.

Just then, Mum and Dad cycled up.

Dad saw Robinson Potts, and stared at
him in astonishment and fury. When Dad
was angry he spoke in a special voice. His
voice reminded Will of bent metal, it had

the same sort of strain to it. In this voice Dad said fiercely, 'What did I say about not going on the mud?' He got off his bike and strode red-faced to where Robinson Potts sat on his bench, pushing muddy hair out of his eyes with a muddy hand, and looking help-

less. From the way Dad looked, Will didn't think he was going to make a big effort to be nice to Robinson Potts. It looked to him as if Dad was going to fly into a fit.

Dad opened his mouth in a shouty sort of way, and Will said quickly, 'I'm very sorry I went on the mud, Dad. We were playing with the ball, and I threw it into the mud by accident, and Robinson helped me get it out again.'

Dad closed his mouth and looked at the ball. The ball was perfectly clean. Dad looked at Will, as if trying to read his mind. Then he looked at Robinson Potts. He nodded slowly, and said, 'I understand.' He didn't say anything else about it, but got back on his bike, and told everyone to hurry up.

Slowly, Robinson Potts got to his feet, opened his mouth as if he was going to say something, shut it again, and climbed back on his bike, looking puzzled.

That evening, after some serious baths, they sat around deciding what they were going to do the next day. After the day's adventure they were all feeling quiet. Robinson Potts hadn't said a word since the incident with the mud. He kept frowning to himself, as if thinking hard about something.

'What do you want to do, Will?' Mum asked.

'Yes, Will,' Dad said. 'Mum and I have been talking, and we think we should do what you want tomorrow.'

Will gave Robinson Potts a little look.

'Well,' he said. 'Perhaps we could go down to the beach here and watch the surfers, and perhaps ask one of them for a go on his board. What do you say, Robinson?'

Everyone looked at Robinson Potts.

'Well, Robinson?' Dad said.

Robinson Potts kept on frowning to himself.

'Robinson?' Mum said sharply.

'No,' Robinson Potts said. 'I don't want to do that.'

Mum made a noise. She also stood up to shout better. But before she could open her mouth, Robinson Potts said quickly, 'I'd rather take you all to my uncle's surf shop down the coast, where we can hire suits and boards free.'

There was a moment's silence while they all repeated these words to themselves. Mum sat down again.

'Really?' she said.

'You're not lying again, are you?' Dad said, a bit rudely.

Robinson Potts shook his head.

'Do you really have an uncle?' Will asked.

Robinson Potts nodded.

'Does he really have a surf shop?' Lucy said.

Robinson Potts nodded again. 'And I really do want to take you,' he said. 'Even if you're not my friend.'

And the funny thing was, he was finally telling the truth.

After the holiday, the Quigleys never saw Robinson Potts again. His mum moved unexpectedly to another city. They didn't miss him, but they did talk about him. It was odd how much they talked about him, as if Robinson Potts had delighted them all, with his disintegrating pyjamas and his loose ankle-bone and his utter ignorance of marine life. A very good thing was that quite a few words that Mum used to use about Will, like 'unhelpful' and 'difficult', became permanently attached to Robinson Potts, and Mum had to think of new words for Will.

But the best thing by far was that Mum and Dad never forgot Will's big effort.

Mum's Big Ride

Mum's Big Ride

A funfair came to town. It wasn't a small
fair. It was massive.

The Quigleys sat in their back room,
talking about it excitedly. The most excited
person was Mum. 'There'll be Waltzers,' she
said. 'And Shunters and Plungers and
Whirlpools.' She grinned. 'All the things
that give you the tummy feeling.'

'What's the tummy feeling?' Lucy asked.

'You know when Dad tosses pancakes?
Well, it's a bit like Dad tossing your
tummy.'

'Is it a nice feeling?'

Mum grinned some more. 'I haven't been
to a funfair for ages, but when I was a girl
I really, really loved it.'

'Will I really, really love it?'

'Tomorrow, we'll go on a ride together,

and you can find out.'

Lucy wrinkled up her face. She wasn't sure about the tummy feeling. 'I'll see,' she said.

'What about rifle arcades?' Will asked. Will didn't like the tummy feeling at all. He liked shooting things and winning prizes.

'I expect there'll be rifle arcades.'

'Good. I'm going to win one of those eight-foot squirrels.'

'Eight-foot squirrels?'

'They always have prizes like that at fairs. Enormous soft toys. Giant teddy bears, monstrously big Babar the Elephants. But the best are the gigantic squirrels. They look sort of cute and sort of mad, and if one toppled onto you it would probably crush you to death,' Will said excitedly.

Dad groaned. Dad didn't like the tummy feeling or eight-foot squirrels.

'We could always stay at home,' he said. 'How about a quiet night in?'

★ ★ ★

The next day, just as it was getting dark,
the Quigleys caught the bus into town.
Usually at that time there weren't many
people about, but tonight the streets were
crowded. The Quigleys went slowly through
the town centre, and turned a corner, and
stopped.

'Look!' Mum said.

They all looked.

'Where's the road gone?' Lucy asked.

The High Street had disappeared below a
mass of rides, arcades, fun-houses, kiosks
and stalls. The fair looked like a whole city
of moving lights. A hubbub of music, shouts
and screams swept up to them.

113

'Wow!' Mum said.

'Double wow!' Lucy said.

'Wow with knobs on,' Will said.

Dad said, 'I don't think we need to stay more than half an hour, do you?'

First, the Quigleys planned what they were going to do. Mum gave Lucy and Will some money of their own to spend. Dad agreed to buy snacks from the stalls.

'Before we start, there are two very important Family Rules,' he said. 'First rule: stay together. I don't want anyone getting lost. If you do get lost, come to this lamppost here. The lamppost is our meeting point. Do you agree?'

They agreed.

'Second rule: no vomiting on big rides. It's messy and embarrassing.'

Mum just laughed. 'I'm never sick on big rides,' she said. 'And I can't wait to go on one.'

The first ride they came to was called the Churner. The Churner looked like the insides of a giant toaster, with two racks of people strapped inside waiting to be toasted. When the music started, the toaster shunted forwards, tilted sideways and suddenly flipped over, and the air was filled with the very odd noises of the people inside.

'Anyone want a go?' Mum asked.

Will shook his head. 'I'd vomit,' he said. 'And that would be breaking one of the Family Rules.'

Dad shook his head. 'I'd die,' he said. 'Which would be breaking one of my own personal rules.'

'What about you, Lucy?'

Lucy watched the Churner for a while. It looked exciting. The people flew sideways, then backwards, then upside-down sideways. But she was nervous.

Mum said temptingly, 'It looks like a good one for the tummy feeling.'

But Lucy couldn't make up her mind, and eventually the Quigleys moved on.

Will scanned the stalls for prize-winning games, and found two straightaway, one with darts and one with Ping-Pong balls.

To win top prize at the darts game you had to score less than five on the special dartboard. Top prize was a nearly life-size fake-fur ostrich with an unpleasant grin.

'I'm so bad at darts I ought to be good at this,' Will said. 'I nearly always score less than five.'

He scored 17, 40, 6 and an unlucky 180.

'That ostrich is putting me off,' he said.

The top prize at the Ping-Pong-ball game was a nearly life-size fake-fur orangutan with insane eyes. To win it you had to score more than five, by bouncing three balls into the right holes.

'Five? I never seem to score less than five.'

He scored zero four times on the trot and

ended on a high with one.

Mum and Dad sympathized.

'Do you know what the problem is?' Will said, suddenly looking cunning. 'I'm too hungry to win anything.'

They bought fried flying fish from a stall selling Caribbean food, and hot pork sandwiches, and quite a lot of pink-and-white nougat, and a tin of chocolate-coated peanuts, and a bunch of green candyfloss, and walked through the fair eating them from the bags. As they went, Mum pointed out rides which Lucy might like.

'The Swooper's good,' she said. 'Very fast. So fast, you sort of leave yourself behind. Do you fancy it?'

Lucy said she wasn't sure.

Dad shuddered.

'Or there's the Backlash. That's a bit like turning your-self inside out.' Mum grinned.

Lucy said she *quite* liked the sound of that.

With his mouth full, Will

118

said, 'Why are you always forcing people to do what they don't want to?'

Mum explained that was what mums did. It was a brief explanation because she was in a good mood. 'Anyway,' she said, 'Lucy *wants* to go on a ride. And there,' she added suddenly, pointing, 'is a ride she would love. My favourite – the Waltzer!'

'What do Waltzers do?' Lucy asked.

'They give you the tummy feeling,' Mum said.

Lucy thought about it. 'OK,' she said. 'I'll go on if you come with me.'

'I'm definitely going on,' Mum said. 'Anyone else?'

Will shook his head.

Dad looked the other way.

Mum and Lucy got into one of the Waltzer cars and sat back and pulled down the metal bar in front of them, and waved at Dad and Will.

Mum said, 'Are you nervous, Poodle?'

Lucy nodded.

'Don't worry. It's going to be fantastic!'

The Waltzer began to move. First they went slowly up and down, like a boat on the waves. Then they went quicker, and started turning round. Soon they began to spin. Mum grinned. Lucy grinned back. A fairground man climbed alongside them and gave them a push, and Lucy suddenly spun so fast she felt her grin stretch. The rest of the fair turned into a blur. Somewhere near, she could hear a bumpy, squeaky noise. The noise went *Oh-oh-oh-oh, a-a-a-argh, nug-ganugganugga.* After a while she realized she was making the noise. Sometimes she spun, sometimes she swung, sometimes she humpbacked up and down, and sometimes she did all these things together, and all the time she had a wonderful, glorious tummy feeling.

Even when the ride was over she couldn't stop grinning. She tried to explain to Will why it was so good, but she couldn't do that either.

'I can't hear what you're saying,' Will said. 'You're grinning too much.'

'It's the tummy feeling,' she said, when she could. 'I can't explain. You'll have to ask Mum.'

But Will wasn't interested in the tummy feeling, and neither was Dad, even though Lucy kept talking about it. They moved off together through the crowds, looking for games with giant-squirrel prizes, and no one noticed that Mum wasn't with them. Mum stayed where she was, leaning on a rail next to the Waltzer. Her face was white and a bit wet, and her hair was stuck to her forehead, and she was holding a hand to her mouth. Mum had just realized that she didn't like the tummy feeling any more.

She groaned to herself and took a deep breath, and tried to think. Someone had to go on rides with Lucy. Dad and Will wouldn't go with her.

It had to be Mum. She took another deep breath.

Dad came back to find her. 'Are you OK?' he asked.

Mum nodded. 'Mmm.'

'Are you sure? You look a bit . . . colourless.'

'Just a bit chilly,' Mum said weakly.

'I wouldn't worry about that. You'll soon warm up when you go on another ride. Come on, we'd better catch up with Will and Lucy.'

The Quigleys walked through the fair, looking at everything. It was a very good fair. All round them people were screaming and laughing as they flew above the street lamps. Lucy kept teasing Dad that he didn't dare go on any of the rides.

They came to a ride called Thrasher.

'This looks like a good one, Mum,' Lucy said. 'Dad wouldn't like it, but I bet you would.'

Mum nodded or, at least moved her head

up and down. 'Wait a second, though,' she said suddenly. 'Isn't that a doughnut stall over there?'

They bought a bag of hot sugared doughnuts, Lucy's favourite, and shared them as they went on. Mum didn't want any.

The next ride they came to was called the Walloper.

'What about that one?' Will said to Lucy. 'You and Mum could go on that. You'd like that, a bit of walloping.'

Lucy agreed. Mum made a noise which didn't mean anything, and looked all round, and at the last second said, 'Oh, look, there's one doughnut left. Who wants the last doughnut?'

While Lucy was eating the last doughnut, they went past half a dozen more rides. But just as they were about to go past the last one, she finished eating, looked up and said, 'I like the sound of this one. Don't you, Mum?'

'Oh,' Mum said, reading the sign. 'The Thrash-Master?' She seemed to go limp. But before she could say anything, Dad said unexpectedly, 'Oh, I wouldn't bother with Thrash-Master.'

'Why?' said Lucy.

'It's a bit feeble, to be honest. Don't you want to go on something fast with me? Something scary and vicious?'

Everyone looked at him, and he looked back at them defiantly. He was fed up with everyone teasing him for not daring to go on scary rides.

'But you don't like anything like that, Dad,' Lucy said.

'Pah! You just watch. We're going to go on the fastest, scariest, most vicious ride here.'

Lucy looked interested. 'Which one, Dad?'

Dad pointed.

Lucy looked. 'Where? I can't see it. Is it behind the Helter-Skelter?

'It *is* the Helter-Skelter,' Dad said, with

triumph. 'And I'm going to go down first. Even though, really,' he added, 'I'm probably too old and might get killed.'

Lucy scowled again.

Will said, 'Dad, even I think the Helter-Skelter's boring.'

Dad explained at length how dangerous the Helter-Skelter was. 'Look,' he said. 'I'm good at the Helter-Skelter. I can come down backwards, head first or reclining on one elbow playing a well-known tune on comb and paper. You've got to want to see that.'

They didn't.

'I'm going anyway,' he said. 'Say goodbye. This might be the last time you see me.'

126

'Goodbye,' Lucy said.

He queued up, got a mat and disappeared, leaving Mum, Will and Lucy waiting at the bottom.

They stood there, watching. Child after child came gently down the Helter-Skelter, slid slowly to the end, and were helped off by a fairground man.

'Where *is* Dad?' Mum said after a while. 'He's taking ages.'

'Perhaps he got nervous when he got to the top,' Will said. 'And couldn't face it.'

At that moment there was a noise from above.

'Someone's shouting,' Lucy said.

'No,' Will said. 'I think it's someone singing.'

'Oh god,' Mum said.

Suddenly Dad came into sight round the last bend, travelling very fast. He was kneeling on his mat, leaning forward in an aggressive racing stance with his hands round his eyes like goggles, singing 'Yes, We Have No Bananas' very loudly. His appearance caused panic among the onlookers at the bottom. The fairground man shouted something. Dad tried to brake. He lost control of his mat, left the slide at speed and sprawled to a stop on the pavement in front of a baby in a pram, who dropped an ice-cream onto Dad's face and burst into tears.

'Actually,' Will said, 'that wasn't bad. No style, but lots of chaos.'

After Dad had made various apologies, they left the Helter-Skelter. Dad said he didn't think a second go would be as good as the first. During the rest of their visit he moved in a painful crouching walk.

'I think I've got burn marks,' he said, wiping his face. 'And that ice-cream got into my eyes.'

'Never mind,' Lucy said. 'Mum and I will cheer you up by going on a big ride and showing you how it's done.'

Mum sighed and looked sad, but before she could say anything, Will said, 'And now, if Dad's finished distracting us I'm going to win an outlandishly big squirrel.'

Mum perked up. 'That,' she said, 'sounds like a great idea.'

'Doesn't it,' Dad said gloomily.

Will and Lucy led the way to the Toss-a-Frog stall.

'I like squirrels,' Lucy said. 'When we've won it, where shall we put it?'

'We can't put it on our beds,' Will said

thoughtfully. 'It's too big, it would break our legs.'

'But it's too big to go in the wardrobe,' Lucy said.

They thought a while.

'I think it needs its own hammock,' Will said at last. 'Dad can make a hammock for it.'

Dad rolled his eyes. 'Fine,' he said. 'And shall I build an en-suite bathroom for it in the corner of the room?'

'That would be nice,' Lucy said. 'Thank you.'

Will started playing Toss-a-Frog. First you put a frog in your dish. Then you aimed the dish. Then you thumped the lever, and the dish shot up. And, if you had aimed properly, the frog flew through the air in a short, graceful arc and landed on a lily pad floating in the middle of the water tank, and stayed there, and didn't slide off one inch to the left or one inch to the right, either of which would disqualify it.

'Nothing to it,' Will said.

It was one pound fifty for three goes.

After he had spent nine pounds, Mum asked him to give up.

'Mum!' Will said. 'I've just been practising till now. You're always telling me to practise things. You're always telling me I'll

never do things properly if I don't practise first. That's what you're always saying. And now I'm practising, and you're telling me to stop.'

'You know that's true, Mum,' Lucy said.

'All right,' Mum said. 'But you have to do it properly soon.'

Will spent another nine pounds.

'Please!' Mum said.

'Just one pound fifty more,' Will pleaded. 'It's for the squirrel. That squirrel's all I've ever wanted.'

They all looked at the squirrel. The squirrel looked back at them. It was eight-foot tall, bright orange and looked ridiculously pleased with itself.

'This is your very last go,' Mum said.

'Pray to god he doesn't actually win it,' Dad said.

For the twenty-fifth time, Will took aim. He missed. He took aim again. He missed again.

'By the way,' Dad said suddenly, 'I know I can't see properly because of all this ice-cream in my eye, but isn't that a rifle arcade over there?'

There was a small commotion, caused by Will abandoning the Toss-a-Frog stall and making his way quickly towards the rifle arcade, followed by Lucy, followed by Mum.

'What about your last go?' Dad shouted after Will.

'Dad says what about your last go?' Lucy said kindly. She often repeated Mum and Dad's questions to Will when he forgot to listen to them.

'Tell him to take it for me!' Will said, as he examined the rifles. 'I'm too busy winning a shooting prize.'

Lucy told him.

Dad sighed. 'I'm don't think I'll bother,' he said to the lady on the Toss-a-Frog stall. 'I don't actually want to win. Anyway, I've been part-blinded by ice-cream.'

'No harm in having a go if you've no chance of winning,' the lady reasoned.

Dad sighed again. 'I suppose you're right,' he said.

At the rifle arcade, Mum, Will and Lucy were having an argument.

'This is too expensive,' Mum said.

'It isn't expensive for something I've always, always wanted to do,' Will said.

'But you're not paying for it,' Mum said.

'That's not the point. The point is that I really, really want to go on it. Just like Lucy really, *really* wants to go on one more big ride,' he added.

'I'd forgotten about one more big ride!' Lucy said, pink with pleasure. 'Thank you, Will.'

Mum, however, hadn't forgotten how bad she felt.

'Just one go then,' she said. 'But take your time,' she added.

The rifle arcade was called 'Wild West Saloon'. There was a counter with a waxwork barman behind it polishing a glass, shelves of bottles, four waxwork cowboys playing cards at a table, a waxwork old man playing an accordion, a birdcage, a piano, a picture of Niagara Falls and a stuffed bear. All these things had little targets on them, and if you hit one the

thing moved or played a tune. It all looked creaky and old-fashioned.

'What do you win?' Will asked the man. 'Is it a squirrel. Or an ostrich?'

The man shook his head. 'If you hit all the targets you win this.' He held out a keyring with a silver bullet on it. 'It's real,' he said. 'No squirrels here.'

Will gasped. 'A real silver bullet,' he said. 'How many targets are there?'

'Ten.'

'How many shots do I have?'

'Fifteen.'

'Has anybody ever done it before?'

'Not tonight.'

'Never mind,' Mum said to the man. 'We'll come back next year.'

Will said, 'Pass me the bullets.'

So it began. Will carefully aimed at the

target on the birdcage, and fired.

Nothing happened.

He fired again. Nothing happened again.

He fired twice more, and still nothing happened.

Lucy put her arm round Will's shoulder to comfort him, and the gun went off, and

a small hole appeared in the canvas roof of the arcade.

'Lucy!' Will said furiously. 'Now you've made me use up all my spare shots! I've got to hit ten targets and I've only got ten shots left.'

Lucy backed away.

Muttering to himself, Will aimed at the birdcage for the sixth time, and fired. After a second's delay, the canary began to sing.

'You hit it!' Lucy cried in surprise. 'You really hit it! Will, you hit it and made it sing!'

'Shh,' Will said in a short, thick voice as he aimed carefully at the stuffed bear. He fired, the bear's jaw dropped open and somewhere in the background there was a hollow growl.

'You hit it again!' Lucy squeaked.

Will didn't bother telling her off this time. He was too busy hitting the targets.

He fired. One of the card-players threw the Ace of Spades into the air.

He fired. The accordionist began to play a tune.

He fired. The picture of Niagara Falls swung sideways on the wall.

Mum and Lucy stood watching him in amazement.

'Got my eye in now,' he said briefly as he reloaded. Then he carried on hitting targets.

At last there was only one target he hadn't hit. It was on the hat of one of the card-players. Will had one shot left.

He aimed, and shuffled a bit, and aimed again. Then he fired.

Nothing happened.

For a second, no one said anything.

Mum said, 'That's really bad luck, Will.'

Will slowly put the gun down. 'I thought I hit it,' he said sadly.

The man on the rifle arcade suddenly stamped his foot on the saloon floor, and there was a bang, and the cowboy's hat flew off.

'Bit stiff, that one,' the man said. 'Needs oiling.' He gave Will his prize. 'Well done. Best shooting tonight.'

'You won!' Lucy said excitedly.

'You won!' Mum said proudly.

'I won?' Will said disbelievingly.

There was a pause while they all stood looking at the silver bullet.

'Well, I told Dad I would,' Will said. 'Didn't I?'

They all looked round. And that's when they realized Dad was lost.

Waiting back at the lamppost, they scanned the crowds for a sign of Dad. But the crowds were thicker now, and it was impossible to see.

'If he got lost, why didn't he come back here, like he said?' Will asked.

'Do you think he went on the Helter-Skelter again?' Lucy said in a small voice. 'And got hurt worse?'

'Or perhaps the ice-cream has totally blinded him,' Will said after a while. 'And he'll never be able to see my silver bullet,' he added sadly.

They waited at the lamppost.

'Look at that man at the lamppost over there, Will,' Lucy said, pointing. 'He's won a giant squirrel.'

The man was bent double under the squirrel, which towered above him, grinning madly.

Will didn't care and said so. '*I've* got a silver bullet,' he said. 'He can keep his squirrel.'

'It's big though, isn't it?'

While they were looking at the squirrel, the man turned round and started walking towards them. 'Oops, wrong lamppost,' the man said.

The man was Dad.

'She said I had no chance of winning,'

Dad went on in a complaining voice. 'She said hardly anyone wins, and anyway I was half blind with ice-cream. And then I won,' he said bitterly. 'It's so unfair. I ought to be able to get my money back.'

After they had all examined the squirrel, and Dad had examined the silver bullet, it was time to go home.

'Here's your squirrel,' Dad said to Will. 'I can't tell you what a relief it is to get rid of it.'

'It's OK,' Will said. 'I don't mind if you carry it. I've got my silver bullet to look after.'

'Wait a minute,' Lucy interrupted. 'You've forgotten.'

'Forgotten what?' Dad said.

'Forgotten my last big ride,' Lucy said. 'And I know exactly which one I want to go on.' She pointed. 'The Churner. And Mum does too.'

Mum looked pale.

'That's what you said,' Lucy said.

Dad looked quite carefully at Mum. 'Poodle,' he said slowly, 'I'm not sure Mum wants to go on the Churner any more.'

Lucy's face scrunched up.

Mum said quickly, 'It's OK. Really,' she said. She took a deep breath. 'I really, really

want to go on the Churner with Lucy.'

Dad looked puzzled. 'Are you sure?' he asked.

'I'm sure.'

'I can't bear to watch,' he said. He went to sit on the steps of the Dodgems, while Mum and Lucy queued for the Churner.

'*Are* you sure?' Lucy asked, looking at Mum.

Mum nodded.

'I could go on my own. I'm tall enough.'

'I know.'

'And I'm brave enough.'

'I know. But you ought to have someone's hand to hold. Just to be comfortable.'

Lucy looked at Mum. Like everyone else, Mum had different faces for different moods, and usually Lucy knew what each of them meant. But this face was odd. It was sort of frozen.

They got near the front of the queue.

Lucy kept looking at Mum. Mum's frozen face was very pale, and a bit damp, and her mouth made Lucy think of feeling sick.

She said, 'Mum? I don't think you want to go on it, do you, Mum?'

Mum didn't say anything.

'Why not? Don't you like the tummy feeling any more?'

Mum shook her head.

Lucy said, 'I don't mind going on my own. Really. I'll sit next to other people so I won't feel lonely.'

'But I don't want you to sit

next to just anyone,' Mum said, as they reached the ticket office. Lucy held Mum's hand, and Mum gave a weak smile. 'I wish there was someone we know who could go on with you,' she said. And at that moment she had an idea. She started talking quickly to the lady in the ticket office, and then she called Will over. 'Quick!' she said. 'Run back to Dad . . .'

'What's going on, Mum?' Lucy asked. 'I don't think Dad can come on the ride with me. He couldn't even do the Helter-Skelter properly.'

'Don't worry,' Mum said. 'He won't need to. I've thought of something else.'

Will and Dad stood by the Dodgems, looking up at the Churner.

'I really don't want to look,' Dad said again.

'Relax,' Will said. 'You're going to like this.'

Now that everyone was strapped into the Churner, it began to move. The row of people rose slowly and fell again, and rose once more. The machine speeded up, and the row of people jerked upwards and fell away, and revolved in a loop.

'I can't see them clearly,' Dad said, squinting. 'I've still got ice-cream in my eye.'

The row of people rose, fell, revolved and flipped sideways at speed.

A number of people standing round Will and Dad began to laugh and point.

'What's going on?' Dad said.

'You'll see,' Will said.

The row of people shot up and hung in the air for a second. And Dad saw.

Strapped into the middle of the row was a chunky girl with bunches and a grin, and strapped in next to her was an eight-foot squirrel.

'My god!' Dad said, rubbing his eyes. 'What *is* Mum wearing?'

It was late when the Quigleys caught the bus home. The bus driver threatened to

charge Dad full fare for the squirrel, and Dad said he'd already paid for it to go on one of the rides.

'It was a good fair, wasn't it?' Mum said.

'It was the best fair ever,' Lucy said. 'I got the tummy feeling, and Will got the silver bullet, and Dad got the cutest little giant squirrel. But what did you get, Mum?'

Mum thought about it.

'I got out of going on the Churner,' she said. 'And perhaps that's the best feeling of all.'

Fatbrain's
Big Adventure

Fatbrain's Big Adventure

Whenever the Peacheys went on holiday they asked the Quigleys to feed their cat, Fatbrain. Fatbrain was big and black and very stupid and sometimes he smelled, but Will and Lucy liked him.

'I don't think he smells,' Lucy said.

'I'm fond of a cat that smells,' Will said. 'And he's so stupid he'd gnaw off his own foot without noticing. But I like that in a cat.'

One day in the summer holidays, Mum and Lucy went over to give Fatbrain his food and water. Dad was in London, and Will was busy reading the *Beano*. In the Peacheys' house, Mum filled Fatbrain's metal dish with cat food and took it outside the back door, and Lucy banged the dish with a spoon. This was the signal for

Fatbrain to come and eat. Usually, after a few minutes, he'd come padding up the garden, looking interested. But this afternoon he didn't appear.

'Bang again,' Mum said.

Lucy banged until her wrist was numb. Still no Fatbrain.

'Do you think he's all right, Mum?' she asked anxiously.

Mum told her not to worry. 'Cats know how to look after themselves.'

Leaving the dish of cat food on the Peacheys' patio, they walked back to their own house. It was a warm afternoon, and they went into their garden for a game of swingball.

'You see,' Mum was saying in a comforting voice, 'Fatbrain may look and smell stupid but actually he's strong and cunning and tough.'

Suddenly Lucy said, 'Look!'

Mum looked. High up on top of the

Quigleys' house, a large black cat was
clinging to the roof, mewing for help.

'Fatbrain!' Mum exclaimed.
'Oh god, he's going to fall
and die!'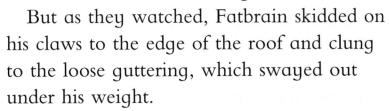

Lucy burst into tears,
and Mum looked embar-
rassed. 'Sorry.' She tried to
think of something else to
say. 'Perhaps he's enjoying
himself,' she said uncertainly.

But as they watched, Fatbrain skidded on
his claws to the edge of the roof and clung
to the loose guttering, which swayed out
under his weight.

'He's not enjoying himself,' Lucy said in a
fierce, unhappy voice. 'He's been exploring,
and he's got stuck on that broken gutter-
thing Dad's always saying he's going to fix
and never does. We have to rescue him.'

Mum saw the urgency of the situation.
'Yes,' she said. 'Yes, we do.'

'How are we going to rescue him?'

Mum thought. 'I'll get Will,' she said.

Will knew what to do straightaway. 'We have to call the fire brigade,' he said. 'So that they can come roaring down the street in a fire-engine with its siren screaming, breaking the wing mirrors off all the parked cars.' He grinned. 'We haven't had a fire engine down our road for ages. Do you realize how lucky we are Fatbrain's got stuck on our roof?'

Mum didn't grin. Mum wasn't keen on Will's idea. 'Isn't there something we can do ourselves?'

They thought.

'The thing is,' Will said, peering up at Fatbrain, 'he's very high up.'

'You don't like high things, do you, Will?' Lucy said. 'You get scared.'

'I could do it,' Will said. 'Or if I couldn't, Dad could, and I could help.'

Mum reminded him that Dad wasn't there.

They all thought some more. 'I've got an idea,' Will said suddenly. He went into the house, and came back a few moments later carrying his catapult.

'What's that, Will?' Mum said.

Will gave her a puzzled look. 'It's a catapult, duh,' he said.

'So?'

'*Cat*apult,' he repeated. 'So obviously it'll be good for shooting cats off roofs.'

After Mum had taken away the catapult, they all stood in the garden thinking again. Above them, Fatbrain was still clinging to the guttering, making small, sad noises.

'Poor Fatbrain,' Lucy said. 'He missed his tea, so he's probably hungry.'

'That's it!' Mum said. 'Food. We can tempt him down with food.'

'Good idea,' Will said. 'Fatbrain's an extremely greedy cat.'

Mum went to get cat food from the Peacheys' house, and a few minutes later, Will appeared in the garden with a tin of cat food in one hand and a spoon in the other. He waved the tin at Fatbrain and banged on it with the spoon. 'This will work for sure,' he said. 'Any minute now, Lucy, you're going to see that cat dive headfirst off the roof into this tin.'

Mum said, 'I think Fatbrain's roof-diving days are over. We need to go closer. You

see how near Fatbrain is to the loft window? If we go up there, we can tempt him closer with the food, and grab him, and pull him through.'

From the loft window they had a much better view of Fatbrain. Or at least of Fatbrain's butt. His butt was balancing half on the roof-tiles, half on the guttering, and it was a very miserable and uncomfortable-looking butt.

'I'm going to tempt him closer now,' Will said.

'Can I tempt him closer too?' Lucy said.

Will shook his head. 'Cats are very sensitive, even greedy ones. You have to speak politely to them.' Will knew a lot about animals, so Lucy had to agree.

He took the tin and leaned as far as he dared out of the window, whispering, 'Here, Pussy, Pussy.'

Fatbrain looked at him blankly, and didn't move.

'He's not moving,' Lucy said. 'Are you being polite enough?'

'I'll use his name,' Will said. 'Fatbrain,' he crooned in a politely musical voice.

That didn't work either.

'Maybe it's not his full name,' Lucy said.

Will thought for a while. 'Numbskull Flab-head Fatbrain,' he said.

'That doesn't sound very polite,' Mum said.

For several minutes, Will waved the tin and crooned politely, and Fatbrain gazed bleakly at it. 'Hey!' Will shouted at last. 'Are you stupid or what? Get your fat butt over here!'

Next Lucy had a go. 'Please, Mister Fatbrain, won't you come in the window, please? Just for a bit.'

Then Mum took the tin, and began to wave it out of the window in large slow sweeps.

'Careful, Mum,' Will said. 'You're meant to be tempting him, not hypnotizing him.'

It made no difference. Fatbrain just stared at them all. The only time he moved was when Will was testing the cat food for flicking and accidentally hit him on the nose. Mum had to explain, very firmly, that they were trying to rescue Fatbrain, not drive him over the edge of the roof to his death.

After that, they all went down to the garden to think again.

Mum said, 'You know, if we could get onto the flat extension roof, we could reach up with a mop or something, and Fatbrain could scramble down onto it.'

'But how can we get up there?' Lucy asked.

'We need a ladder. We had one, but I think we threw it away.'

'No, we didn't,' Will said. 'Dad put it somewhere.'

They found it lying along the wall of the passageway, an old-fashioned, heavy ladder of dark wood, and pulled it out to take a closer look.

'It's old,' Mum said doubtfully. 'Perhaps it's rotten.'

Will disagreed. 'It's a bit old, but it's a good ladder,' he said. He tried to lift it. 'You can tell it's good because it's so heavy.' He grinned. 'They don't make ladders like this any more.'

They all tried to lift it. 'It *is* heavy,' Mum said. 'Are we going to be able to manage it?'

It took them five minutes to carry the ladder ten yards to the patio, and another five minutes to haul it upright against the

extension wall. The ladder was very heavy
and moist, and soft in places, but Will
insisted it was a good ladder, and Lucy said
it was their only ladder, and in the end
Mum agreed to use it.

'Wish me luck,' Will said.

'I'm not letting you go,' Mum said. 'If it's
risky, I'll go.'

Will argued bitterly about risks and how
much he liked them, but Lucy helpfully
reminded him that he was scared of heights,
and, in any case, Mum was firm. Mum
could be very firm. You could tell because
of her eyes. She gave a deep breath and got
onto the ladder herself.

'I don't like this much,' she called down

after a while, clinging to the wet sides.
'How far up am I now?'

'You've still got your foot on the bottom rung.'

She opened her eyes, and began to climb. The children made encouraging noises like, 'Good, Mum, now the other foot again!' and 'Hurry up, Mum, or the cat food will have gone off by the time you get there!' When she finally reached the extension roof, Will and Lucy began to caper round the patio whooping. But they whooped too soon.

As Mum was pulling herself onto the roof, she accidentally pushed the ladder sideways with her foot, and felt it shift sluggishly beneath her.

Will and Lucy gasped.

'Oh, help!' Mum cried. She kicked out for support, and the ladder began to slide away.

'Mum!' Will and Lucy cried together.

'Oh, look out, look out, look out!' she yelled. She thrashed once like a swimmer in mid-air, and wriggled tummy-first onto the

roof, and the ladder
teetered creakily
along the wall and
fell suddenly with a
bang onto the patio.

Will was the first to
recover from the shock.
'That was great,' he
said. 'I want to do that.
It's my turn to do it
next.'

Mum looked down,
white-faced, from the
extension roof. 'Are
you two all right?' she
asked anxiously. Will,
already busy with the
ladder, didn't answer.

Lucy said, 'I'm all right. Are you all
right, Mum?'

Mum nodded, a little shakily.

'Come on, Lucy,' Will said. 'Don't just
stand there chatting. Help me get the ladder
up. It's my go next, then you can have a

turn.' Together they pulled heroically at the enormous ladder. But they couldn't lift it. 'It's no good,' Will said, panting. 'Come on, Mum, you have to help too. Mum?'

He looked up at Mum. Mum was sitting on the extension roof with her arms folded, looking down at him. 'Oh,' he said. 'I forgot. You're stuck up there.'

There was a small silence while they thought about this. Lucy almost began to cry, but she stopped herself enough to say, in a small voice, 'I don't like Mum being stuck up there.'

Will held her hand. 'Don't worry,' he said kindly. 'We're going to get her down. You'll see.' He looked up at Mum. 'What's their number?' he called.

'Whose number?'

'The fire brigade.'

Mum said that she didn't want Will to call the fire brigade, not even to be rescued herself. 'I know what you can do,' she said. 'You can go round to some of our friends to ask for help lifting the ladder.'

'Will you be OK while we're gone?' Lucy asked.

Mum nodded, and looked at Will. Will took charge. 'Come on, Lucy,' he said briskly. 'We don't want to leave Mum up there all day.'

While they were gone, Mum sat on the roof alone, thinking. She wasn't scared any more. She felt sure that Will and Lucy would help get her down. They were sensible children. Will could be a bit dreamy, and Lucy was stubborn sometimes, but they were both kind-hearted and thoughtful. Some days, it was true, all she ever seemed to do was tell them not to be so loud, or ask them to tidy their room, or stop doing cartwheels in the kitchen. But in fact there were just as many nice moments, which were somehow easier to forget. She smiled to herself. Stuck up on the extension roof, waiting to be rescued, she felt oddly lucky. She drew her knees up to her chest, and looked across the back gardens lit up in the afternoon sun,

and told herself that in future she would
remember the nice moments too.

Will and Lucy went down the street. They
went past the blind lady's house, and the
house with the sparrow bush, and the house
which builders were repairing.

'It's funny, isn't it,' Will said, 'the way
Mum didn't like climbing the ladder. Do
you think she's scared of heights?'

'I don't know,' Lucy said. 'What's it like

being scared of them?'

Will thought about it. 'Do you remember that rice pudding Dad made with cayenne pepper once?'

Lucy shuddered.

'Well, it's a bit like that. Your insides feel wrong.'

They came to Gary and Elena's house, and knocked on the door, but there was no answer. At the end of the street, they tried at Ted and Sally's, but they were out too. 'Haven't they gone to stay with their grandma and grandpa?' Lucy said.

They tried three more houses, but no one was in. At the last house, a babysitter

answered the door, and told them that it was the Woodcraft folks' annual barbecue in the park.

'That's why so many people are out,' Lucy said to Will. 'What shall we do now?'

Will put his hands in his pockets to think. He usually found it easier thinking with his hands in his pockets, it made him feel cunning. Sometimes, though, he was distracted by things he found in his pockets. Today he discovered a rubber band, fifty pence, a dead battery, a crisp packet and one of Mum's back teeth which he was going to swap at school. He spent a few minutes examining them all with great interest, especially the fifty pence piece.

'What can you buy for fifty pence?' he asked out loud.

'Sweets,' Lucy said promptly. She liked sweets. 'From the sweet shop round the corner.'

'What sort of sweets?'

Lucy said, 'Oh, I don't know, gobstoppers, Refreshers, white mice, Black Jacks,

Fruit Salads, liquorice string, sherbet foun-
tains, jelly beans, Toffos, flying saucers,
Freddo frogs.'

'OK,' Will said. 'Let's go.'

Mum was getting quite chilly on the
extension roof when Will and Lucy got
back. She knew they were back because she
heard the front door shut. Then she heard
them talking. Then she heard them put on
the television. They didn't come out to the
patio though. In the end she had to call
them, and Will and Lucy came out with
their mouths full and looked up at her
curiously.

'Oh!' they said. It was quite a shock to
see Mum still up there.

'Couldn't you get down?' Will asked.

Mum gave them a look, and suddenly
they felt very embarrassed. They both
began to explain different things at the
same time.

Mum interrupted them. 'Never mind. The
problem is, I'm still stuck here.'

Will and Lucy were just thinking about this when they heard a key turn in the front door, and Dad appeared, looking battered. He often looked battered when he'd been to London. It was the trains, he said, that did the battering. The children ran loudly towards him.

'Hello,' he said wearily. 'I'm glad to see you too.'

'No, you don't understand,' Will said.

'You don't,' Lucy said. 'We're *really* glad to see you. And so is Mum.'

Dad stood on the patio and looked up at Mum, and Mum sat on the extension roof looking down at him, and Dad began to laugh.

'What's funny?' Mum said.

'You're so good to me,' Dad said. 'I've had such a hard day in London, and the trains were so bad, but you always know how to cheer me up.'

Will and Lucy began to explain.

'What do you mean, Fatbrain's stuck?' Dad said. He pointed, and they turned round and found Fatbrain sitting on the patio, cleaning a paw. He sat there in a comfortable way, as if he'd never been up on the roof at all. From time to time he looked pityingly up at Mum on the extension roof.

'Fatbrain!' Lucy cried.

'Flab-head!' Will cried.

'Now you know why I don't like cats,' Dad said.

An argument began about cats, which was interrupted by Mum. 'Excuse me!' she said crossly. 'Would some-

body mind getting me down?' She said 'somebody' but she was looking at Dad.

Dad took off his jacket.

'Be careful, though,' Mum added. 'The ladder's heavy.'

Dad paid no attention to this. 'I think I can manage to lift up a ladder,' he said.

Five minutes later, after a lot of heaving and some swearing, and the sort of help from the children that made the ladder seem heavier, Dad eventually got it into position. 'It *is* heavy,' he panted. 'But it's a good ladder. They don't make ladders like this any more.'

Will and Lucy grinned.

'And now,' Dad said to them. 'Watch carefully. This is how you do a rescue.'

He sprang lightly onto the ladder and began to climb, and when he was halfway up, it split down the middle with a tremendous crack, and left him hanging from the eaves of the extension roof. The two halves of the ladder fell sideways and smashed through the hanging baskets. There

was a noise like the sudden roaring of a
crowd, which Dad made all on his own,
and the next second he was lying next to
Mum on the extension roof, gasping and
groaning.

'Good rescue,' Mum said.

Dad made a face. 'Bloody ladder,' he
said. 'Thank God they don't make them
like that any more.'

After Will and Lucy had got over their

astonishment, they did a little dance on the patio because having Mum and Dad stuck on the roof was the most exciting thing that had happened in ages. And besides, as Will said, they definitely had to get the fire brigade now. 'I ought to phone Dani and Matt first,' he said thoughtfully, 'so they can come and watch the fire engine smash its way down the street.'

But Lucy wasn't sure. 'Mum didn't want us to get the fire engine,' she said. Will began to argue, but she added, 'And we have to make up for forgetting about her before, when we went to the sweet shop by mistake.'

Will looked ashamed. 'All right,' he said glumly. 'Only I hope you can think of some good ideas.' He shouted up to Mum and Dad, 'We're going to get you down, but you have to wait a bit while we think of good ideas. It's Lucy's turn to think first.'

Dad rolled his eyes. 'Just go round to one of our friends' and get help,' he shouted back.

Mum explained that all their friends were

out for the evening. 'Let Will and Lucy think for a while,' she said. 'I'm sure they'll come up with something sensible.'

Dad made a short, loud noise to show he disagreed, and Mum and Dad began to argue among themselves, while Will and Lucy sat on the lawn taking it in turns to think of sensible ideas.

'We could fill up the paddling pool so they could jump into it,' Will said.

'That's not a sensible idea,' Lucy said.

'What sort of idea is it then?' Will asked sharply.

'It's a very damp idea,' Lucy said. 'I've got a better one. We can make a pile of things, like the garden furniture and the barbecue set and the lawnmower, and climb up it.'

But Will thought Lucy's idea too wobbly.

Fatbrain came to sit in Lucy's lap, and they stroked him thoughtfully while they concentrated.

'What about tempting them down with smells, like we tried to do with Fatbrain?' Will suggested. 'Bacon, say, or lasagne. Once they get hungry, they'll find a way down by themselves.'

They both thought this was a good idea, but too slow, so they thought some more.

In the meantime, Mum and Dad sat on the roof watching them. 'You can tell they're being sensible by how thoughtful they look,' Mum said, and Dad replied, quite forcefully, that he was prepared to bet a goodish amount of money that any ideas they had would be mad and possibly dangerous.

Just then, Will shouted up to them. 'We've thought of an idea now.'

'I thought of it,' Lucy added.

'Lucy thought of it first,' Will said. 'And I thought it was good, which is like thinking of it second. Anyway, it needs both of us to do it, so we're going now, and we'll be back soon.' And before Mum and Dad could say anything, they disappeared. The front door banged once, then everything was quiet.

'Oh,' Mum said.

'Exactly,' said Dad. 'I'd better see if that drainpipe will take my weight.'

But before he had a chance, the front door banged again and Will and Lucy came onto the patio carrying a smart aluminium ladder of just the right height and weight.

Dad gasped.

'Your money's mine,' Mum said.

'But,' Dad said in a distracted way, 'I thought you said all our friends were out for the evening.'

'They are,' Lucy said.

'Then where did you get that ladder?' he asked. He thought for a minute. 'You didn't steal it, did you?'

Lucy explained that the ladder belonged to the builders in the street. 'I saw it before,' she said. 'And I forgot it for a bit because of the sweets. And afterwards I remembered it again.'

'I helped her remember it,' Will said.

'Once we'd remembered it, it was easy,' Lucy said. 'We just had to ask them to borrow it because of our emergency of being stuck on the roof.'

'It's funny isn't it,' Will said. 'The way hard things sometimes turn into easy things. I don't really understand it.'

'It's because of being sensible,' Lucy said.

Mum beamed. Dad said, a little

nervously, 'By the way, did you tell the builders who was stuck on the roof?'

'We said our ball was stuck,' Lucy said promptly. 'Because, Dad, if we'd said our mum and dad were stuck, they would have thought you were a bit stupid. So we were quite kind.'

Dad looked relieved. 'Thanks, Poodle,' he said.

Mum and Dad came down the ladder.

'I knew you'd be sensible,' Mum said, to Will and Lucy.

Dad examined the builder's ladder. 'A bit flimsy,' he said. 'But not bad.'

They had a family hug on the patio.

'I'm glad we're rescued,' Dad said. 'I think there's some beer in the fridge.'

'I'm glad too,' Mum said. 'I could do with a beer.'

'Fatbrain's glad too,' Lucy said.

They all looked round the patio for him.

'Where's that fat-brained cat got to now?' Dad said.

There was a sudden noise above them,

and, as they looked up, Fatbrain appeared
on the roof, skidded onto the loose guttering
and began mewing for help.

The End

Dad

Mum

L

um

Lucy

Will

Dad

Mum

L

um

Lucy

Will

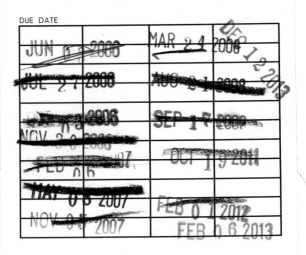